jF BAPTIST Kelly
Isaiah Dunn is my hero /
Baptist, Kelly J.,

ISAIAH DUNN IS MY HERO

ISAIAH DUNN IS MY HERO

KELLY J. BAPTIST

CROWN BOOKS FOR YOUNG READERS
New York

Text copyright © 2020 by Kelly J. Baptist
Jacket art copyright © 2020 by Lacy Jordan

All rights reserved. Published in the United States by Crown Books for Young Readers, an imprint of Random House Children's Books, a division of Penguin Random House LLC, New York.

Crown and the colophon are registered trademarks of Penguin Random House LLC.

Visit us on the Web! rhcbooks.com

Educators and librarians, for a variety of teaching tools, visit us at RHTeachersLibrarians.com

Library of Congress Cataloging-in-Publication Data is available upon request.
ISBN 978-0-593-12136-8 (trade) — ISBN 978-0-593-12137-5 (lib. bdg.) — ISBN 978-0-593-12138-2 (ebook)

The text of this book is set in 11-point Adobe Text Pro.
Interior design by Cathy Bobak

Printed in the United States of America
10 9 8 7 6 5 4 3 2 1
First Edition

For the students of Benton Harbor Area Schools—
you are my heroes!

March 1

WE ARE *SOOO* not supposed to be here.

I know it the second the door to P.J.'s dings when we open it, but I can't just leave my best friend, Sneaky, hanging, so I walk in behind him, my stomach karate-chopping the whole time.

Sneaky acts like he's been here before, which he probably has. I've only heard horror stories. P.J.'s Liquor Spot is a little store on the corner of 5th and Creighton, and if you know anything about Creighton, you know that something bad's always happening there. Like, every week. Sneaky's mom and mine always tell us to stay away, even though P.J.'s has the cheapest candy and ice cream bars. For the most part, I listen. Sneaky doesn't.

"Yo, hurry up," I say to Sneaky in a whisper, noticing some older kids watching us with narrowed eyes.

As if being on Creighton isn't bad enough, P.J.'s is also kinda dark inside, and not that clean. The music playing makes me feel mad for no reason, and a frown inches across my face.

I follow Sneaky to the candy aisle, which is right near the front counter. While I keep glancing around, Sneaky studies the candy bars, taking his time when we need to get outta here!

"Aight, 'Saiah, get six Snickers and six Milky Ways," Sneaky says, reaching for Skittles and Starburst.

I grab what he says, and some bubble gum, too.

"Mike O wanted gum yesterday, remember?" I say.

"Oh yeah! Good look, bro." Sneaky grabs some packs of M&M's, and I get Butterfingers and Laffy Taffy. By now, our arms are pretty full.

"Some 3 Musketeers?" I ask, but I don't get an answer.

Bam! Bam!

I almost drop all the candy on the ground when the guy at the register bangs on the counter to get our attention.

"Hey, candy man," he calls, nodding at our stash. "Y'all got money for all that?"

"Yeah," says Sneaky, walking to the counter. The guy studies us to make sure we don't try to slip anything into our pockets or backpacks. We dump everything on the counter and the guy starts ringing it up.

"Eight thirty-five," he says, putting the candy into a bag but not handing it over until Sneaky gives him the money. Eight dollars and thirty-five cents exactly. Sneaky don't play when it comes to his candy business and his money.

The guy slides the bag toward Sneaky, and he puts it into his backpack before we walk out.

"That place is crazy!" I say, breathing a sigh of relief, but Sneaky doesn't notice.

"Yo, I'll make, like, a fifteen-dollar profit once I sell this," he says, all excited. "See, that's why I come here."

Sneaky's definitely right about the candy prices in P.J.'s. But when I hear the door ding again and glance over my shoulder, I wish we had just gotten our candy at the 7-Eleven near Sneaky's house.

I stop walking, and so does Sneaky, trying to figure out what I'm staring at.

"What?" he asks.

"Nothing," I say. I have to force myself to turn around and keep walking, instead of racing back to P.J.'s. "Thought some of those dudes were coming for us."

Sneaky sucks his teeth. "Man, forget them. They're not gonna do nothing to us."

I don't remind him that a kid got jumped over here just last week, or that Creighton schools are our rivals. I'm too busy thinking about other things.

Like how I just saw Mama go into P.J.'s, and how I know exactly what she'll come out with.

March 2

MAMA SAYS I always liked words; that I was talking before I could walk, and reading and writing before I even got to kindergarten. For some reason, I like poems. Nobody knows that except Mama and Daddy, and maybe Charlie, my little sister. Sneaky knows a lot about me, but he don't know that.

According to Mama, I get my love of words from my daddy, who wrote tons of stories in his notebooks. I like making words fit together like puzzle pieces, and coming up with the perfect rhyme. But since Daddy died four months ago, nothing fits and nothing rhymes, no matter how hard I try to make it.

Mama didn't do very well after Daddy died, and neither did me and Charlie, I guess. But at least me and Charlie started to have some sunny days after a while. Mama's been all rain. She started missing days at work, and then she stopped going at all. The less she went to work, the more bottles started showing up around our apartment, like long-lost cousins who never leave, all of 'em with the labels torn off. Mama probably thinks I don't know what she's drinking, but I do. And I know it's only making things worse—so bad, we couldn't live in our apartment anymore.

Today is Day 17 in the Smoky Inn, which is what I call the motel we've been staying in. It's really called the Sleep Inn Motel, but everything smells like smoke, so they should really change the name. Most of the time, Mama lays in bed all day, which means I have to look out for Charlie, who's four and pretty annoying. Like right now, she just drew these *pink* flowers in my notebook, the one I used to write all my poems in.

"Look, 'Saiah!" Charlie says, like I'm supposed to be excited that she drew over my poem about rain.

Rain is just like tears from the sky.
Cuz even things up high have to cry.

"Charlie, why'd you do that?" I say, snatching the notebook from her.

"Cuz," she says, shrugging and bouncing off to the bed she shares with Mama. Mama doesn't even stir when Charlie jumps on the bed, and she doesn't say anything when I tell Charlie to leave my stuff alone.

"But you don't write in it, 'Saiah," Charlie says, sucking on two fingers, her most disgusting habit.

Charlie's right, though. I haven't written one word this year. Every time I try to, it's like the words freeze in my brain, which makes the lead freeze in my pencil. Nothing comes out.

I flip through the pages in my notebook, and half of them are blank. Wonder why Charlie didn't at least draw on an empty page.

Clouds are the Kleenex to wipe the sky's face.
They move away quick when the sun gets in place.

Other than the scribbles all over it now, it's a pretty good poem. There's a pen on the raggedy motel table; I reach for it and turn to a blank page.

"You gonna write something about me, 'Saiah?" Charlie calls.

"No," I say.

I stare at the page, but no words come out. Ten minutes later, when I need to leave for school and Charlie starts whining that she's hungry, my page looks exactly the same.

Empty.

March 4

SNEAKY'S SNORING IS like thunder trapped in a blender. No matter how tight I squeeze the pillow around my head, it's still loud.

I heard you should nudge a snoring person, and that'll make them stop. I kick Sneaky, like, three times, and it doesn't work!

The room is dark, but it's that half dark/half light that means it's about 7:06, way too early to be awake after staying up till 3 a.m.

Sneak turns over, farts, and keeps snoring, and that's when I know I won't be getting any more zzz's. I pull the pillow off my head and sit up. Sneaky's room is small, and he shares it with his big brother, Antwan, who's pretty much a jerk. But it beats being stuck in that smoky motel room. If it was up to me, I'd probably live with Sneaky, instead of just spending the weekend with him, which I had to beg Mama to do.

I reach for my backpack and pull out my daddy's gold notebook, which I've been reading, like, every day since I found it when we still lived in our apartment. I keep his notebook next to mine in my backpack. Guess I'm thinking his words might jump over to my notebook if I keep them close to each other. Unlike me, Daddy filled his notebook from beginning to end with his thoughts about things, but mostly with stories called "The Beans and Rice Chronicles of Isaiah Dunn." In the stories, a ten-year-old kid superhero named Isaiah Dunn goes on tons of secret missions and gets his power from bowls of beans and rice. When I first found Daddy's notebook, I thought it was cool that he wrote about me as a superhero. I wish all the beans and rice Mama's been making would give me some type of superpower in real life.

I count sixty-four pages left to read in Daddy's notebook, which seems like a lot, but if I keep reading every day, I'll be done in no time. That makes me read extra slow. I don't wanna think about what will happen when I get to the end. Daddy should've written "Isaiah Dunn and the Never-Ending Tale," where the notebook has magic powers to keep the story going forever. In the story I'm reading now, Isaiah Dunn races against the clock to find a clue hidden in a box of cereal at the grocery store.

The grocery store part makes me think about Mama, and I stop reading. I wonder what she's doing right now, and if Charlie is with her. I think Charlie hates being in the motel as much as I do, and I feel a little guilty for leaving her alone for the weekend. I'm thinking maybe if we get enough money, we can find a real nice place to live, and then Mama would feel better. I know I would.

I flip to the page in Daddy's notebook where he wrote about fears. He wrote that when you name a fear, it becomes defeatable, and he put down some of his fears. Some of them are funny, like "octopuses" and "fire hydrants" and "wasps." Others are scary, like "wolves" and "burglars" and "our car going off a bridge into deep water." I'm scared of daddy long-leg spiders, tsunamis, and sometimes dogs. I write those down next to Daddy's list. Then I add: *eating beans and rice every day, not being able to write poems,* and *having to live at Smoky Inn forever.* My last fear is the worst one. *Losing Mama, too.*

I reach down to the bottom of my backpack for my stash of money, which I keep in one of Daddy's old socks. I empty the sock out and count all the change and dollar bills: $19.78. Nowhere near enough to get us a sweet apartment.

I keep reading, hoping that maybe I'll find a money-making idea from the story, but my eyes get super heavy, and the next thing I know, Sneaky's nudging me.

"Yo, wake up, Mr. Librarian!" He smirks.

The room's completely light now, and my neck is sore from how I fell asleep.

"Okay, Sir Snores," I say back. I put Daddy's notebook in my backpack before Sneaky can clown me for what I'm reading. He'd definitely clown me for my book of poems.

"Whatever," Sneaky says. "I don't snore."

I shake my head. No use arguing with him. If I had a phone, I'd just record him or something.

"You hungry?" Sneaky asks, reaching for his PlayStation controller. He'd play for hours without even thinking about breakfast, but not me.

"Yeah," I say, and my stomach rumbles automatically. Sneaky's mom actually makes real breakfast, like, every day, and I'm catching a whiff of goodness right now! I beat Sneaky to the kitchen, and when I get there, I see a stack of pancakes on the table—golden brown, not burnt and lumpy like the ones Mama makes at Smoky Inn. Right next to the pancakes is a plate of perfectly crispy bacon, and Sneaky's mom is scrambling eggs at the stove. Everything smells so good, my stomach rumbles again.

Sneaky's mom takes one look at us and makes a face.

"Uh-uh," she says. "Y'all can take your stank-breath, crusty faces to the bathroom before you sit at my table."

"Ma, c'mon!" whines Sneaky, walking closer to her.

"Sneaky, don't play with me!" she says, holding a hand in front of her nose, like he smells so bad it might mess up her face. "And, Isaiah, you not a guest; you know the drill."

I don't stick around complaining, just go to the bathroom and get my toothbrush from where I always keep it, in the second drawer on the right. I brush, use mouthwash, and wash my face with a cloth that smells just like the Laundromat on Michigan Avenue.

"That's better," Sneaky's mom says when I come back to the kitchen. "Go 'head and fix a plate."

By the time Sneaky wanders back in, I already have butter and syrup on the pancakes.

"So what are you guys doing today?" asks Sneaky's mom, like she always does at breakfast. Me and Sneaky lock eyes, and we both talk at the same time.

"We gotta clean up the room," Sneaky says.

"And maybe go to the park," I add.

"Plus, 'Saiah's gonna test me on my spelling words," Sneaky says.

See, we learned real quick that if we don't have a plan, and just shrug and say "I dunno" when Sneaky's mom asks what we're doing, then she'll have us sweeping, scrubbing walls, wiping down the windows, and other weird chores.

"Um-hmm." Sneaky's mom gives us a look like she kinda believes us, kinda doesn't. "Well, y'all can pick up a few things for me from the store when you go out, okay, Sneaky?"

"Uh-huh." Sneaky's mouth is full of pancake, so I add, "We can do that, no problem."

"Thank you, Isaiah." Sneaky's mom pats my arm. "*Somebody* knows the right way to answer a question around here."

She stands, thumps Sneaky on the head, and walks out of the kitchen with her food.

"Make sure y'all wash your plates!" she calls.

"Dude, we gotta bounce before she makes us do laundry or something," Sneaky says, taking his plate to the sink. I grab another pancake and pour syrup over it. No way am I passing up seconds.

Once we're done washing our plates, we head to Sneaky's room to clean up, but we end up playing Madden NFL on his PlayStation instead.

"Taste the turf!" Sneaky yells when he sacks my quarterback, and it wakes Antwan up.

"Yo, shut up!" Antwan growls, throwing a pillow that hits both of us in the face. Sneaky throws the pillow back, and turns the volume down on the TV.

But when Sneaky's running back fumbles a few minutes later, and I scoop the ball up and run for a touchdown, I forget all about Antwan and jump up screaming. Problem is, Antwan jumps up, too, and his eyes are a scary red.

"Didn't I tell y'all to shut up?" he says, adding in a few cuss words this time. I sit back down, feeling a little nervous. Antwan turned into a different kind of dude once he started high school this year, and Sneaky's mom is always fussing with him about who he hangs out with and how he treats Sneaky.

"Yo, Sneaky, you and yo' punk friend need to get outta here."

Antwan glares at us. The room is small enough to smell Antwan's funky breath. A year ago, me and Sneaky would've clowned him about it. But right now, Sneaky just sucks his teeth and turns the PlayStation off.

"Whatever," he says to his brother, then to me, "Yo, Isaiah, let's go to the park, and let this dummy clean the room."

I pull on a T-shirt, lace up my sneakers, and we get out of there before Antwan thinks too hard about that last sentence.

March 5

IT'S SUNDAY NIGHT, 7:08 p.m. Mama was supposed to pick me up at three. Sneaky's mom's been calling her, but no answer.

"Do y'all have a house phone where y'all staying?" Sneaky's mom asks.

"Um, I don't know it," I say, staring at my shoes. Sneaky's the only one who knows we moved into a motel, not an apartment on the other side of the city, and I made him promise not to tell anybody.

"You don't know your phone number?" Sneaky's mom asks, and I can tell she's a tiny bit pissed.

"Ma, c'mon!" Sneaky says, glancing at me. "Nobody uses house phones anymore."

Truth is, there's a phone in our room, and Mama even told me the number. But I made sure it slipped out of my brain like the water from our leaky faucet. That room is *not* home.

"Maybe she's down at Miz Rita's," I say, mainly because it's the first thing that pops into my mind.

"We'll go check," Sneaky says, pulling my arm.

Once we're in the hallway, he asks, "You really think she's down there?"

"I don't know," I tell him. "Maybe Charlie's getting her hair done or something."

If Mama has a whole lotta bad days in a row, Charlie ends up with her hair in this crazy Afro puff that doesn't get combed. When we still lived in this building, Miz Rita would be the one to hook Charlie up with braids and beads and stuff. I'm hoping she's hooking Charlie's hair up right now, and that Mama's there, too, maybe even laughing with Miz Rita.

The elevator's broken, so we take the stairs to the first floor and knock on Miz Rita's door.

"Uh-oh," she says when she opens it, "trouble's at my door."

"Hey, Miz Rita," we say.

"Is my mama here?" I ask. "Or Charlie?"

Miz Rita frowns a little. "No, I haven't seen either one since y'all moved." Miz Rita gives me a look. "Matter fact, not one of you even came to tell me you were leaving! Had to find out from Sneaky!"

My eyes drop to my shoes again. Miz Rita's right; we haven't been back to the building since we had to leave last month. We didn't even tell anyone goodbye. I don't think Mama wanted anyone to know that she couldn't pay the rent anymore.

"Isaiah?" Miz Rita says my name in a way that forces me to look at her. "Is everything okay, baby?"

"We're good," I tell her, cuz I've gotten used to saying that, even when we're not.

"Well, you tell your mama and little Miss Charlie that I miss them, all right?"

"I will."

"And you stay outta trouble, Sneaky, you hear?"

Sneaky grins. "Miz Rita, I'm never in trouble!"

"Uh-huh," she says, rolling her eyes. She tells us good night, and we start back up the stairs. When we get to the seventh floor, Sneaky stops. I do, too. Seventh floor is my floor. *Was* my floor. I used to wish we lived at the very top, like Sneaky, but Daddy always said there was something special about the number seven.

"Ever wonder who lives in your place now?" asks Sneaky.

I shrug. "I don't know. Maybe sometimes."

"Let's go see," Sneaky says, and his hand pushes the door open before I can think of a reason to stop him.

"What we gonna say?" I whisper once we're in front of 722.

Sneaky shrugs and knocks on the door. I'm thinking we'll probably have to bolt when the door opens, but we both just stand still.

An Asian dude, maybe, like, seventeen, opens the door.

"Hi," says Sneaky. "We're collecting pop bottles for school. Do you have any empty ones?"

The kid stares at us for a second, and even though I know he has no idea who I am, it kinda feels like he does.

"No, we don't have any," he says. A shorter woman, probably his mom, comes behind him and says something in their language. The kid waves his hand and answers her.

While they're doing that, I look inside the apartment, and it's all different. They got the TV in a totally different spot, and their couch doesn't look as comfy as ours. They probably don't know that I once threw up right in the hallway, or that Charlie drew purple crayon all over the wall in the living room.

They don't know any of that. To them, we're just two kids collecting pop bottles. And they don't have any to give us.

"I liked it better when y'all was there," Sneaky says as we walk back upstairs to his place.

"Me too."

I wonder what Mama would think about the aquarium they have in our old apartment. She always told us, "No pets!" Daddy probably wouldn't like the new paintings on the walls. He liked to hang up sports stuff.

When I'm back in Sneaky's room, and I'm holding Daddy's notebook, I wonder if he knew something was gonna happen to him; if he knew I'd have to be a hero for real, and that's why he wrote the stories he did. One thing's for sure; when I don't write, it feels like I'm letting him down.

March 11

"'SAIAH, WHAT'S this?"

I pry my eyes open and squint up at Charlie, who has something so close to my face, I can't see what it is.

"Dang, move back!" I say, pushing her hand and blinking the sleep away. Charlie's got this annoying habit of waking me up by being right in my face and super loud. At Smoky Inn, I sleep on a tiny couch pull-out that creaks every time I move, and definitely every time Charlie jumps on it.

Charlie moves back an inch, which doesn't help too much. I sit up, and she holds out her hand again. When I look down, my stomach starts doing its karate-chopping, and I glare at Mama, who's still bundled up under the covers on her side of the bed. I want to tell Charlie to go ask Mama what it is, but I know I can't.

"Is it bad?" Charlie asks.

I take the label from her and study it, trying to think up something to tell her.

"I don't know, Charlie," I say. "Where'd you get this?"

"It was in our bed," Charlie says, pointing to her spot by Mama.

I get a little mad that Mama would rip off the label from her bottle and leave it in the bed for Charlie to find. She should be the one answering Charlie's questions, not me!

"I think it's trash," I tell Charlie, talking louder than I have to, hoping Mama hears. "It's a wrapper from something, and it needs to get thrown away."

"Oh," says Charlie. She skips over to her side of the bed, reaches under her pillow, and brings me a whole handful of torn-off labels. "Is this trash, too?"

I snatch them from her hand and crumple them up.

"Hey, don't snatch, 'Saiah!" Charlie pouts. "Those are mine!"

"No, they're not!" I yell. "These aren't for you!"

My voice wakes Mama, and she sits up groggily.

"Isaiah, what are you yelling for? I'm trying to get some rest!"

I want to show Mama what Charlie found, want to throw the labels right in front of her and see how she explains herself. I want to tell her I saw her receipt to P.J.'s in the refrigerator, stuck to the empty carton of orange juice. But instead, I squeeze the labels tighter in my hand and try to ignore the karate-chopping in my stomach.

"Mama—" Charlie starts to say, but I cut her off.

"Let's get some breakfast, Charlie," I tell her.

"Yeah, let your brother get you cereal or something. . . ." Mama's voice trails off as she settles back into her cocoon.

Cocoon is a funny word. I wrote a poem about it once, still remember it by heart:

One day I'll build a cocoon on the moon, and
*   when I come out,*
I'll eat clouds with a spoon!

I remember showing Daddy that one, and he laughed. "Well, that would be something, wouldn't it, 'Saiah?" he said. "Clouds with a spoon."

Today, it's just cereal with a spoon. Nasty cereal, too. I think about the Froot Loops and Frosted Flakes on top of Sneaky's refrigerator and wish the boxes could magically transport to our table. Also, there's barely enough milk for both of us, so I mix some faucet water in the jug when Charlie's not looking and shake it up real good.

"Here," I say, plopping the bowls on the tiny, wobbly table in the kitchen area.

Charlie slurps the milk like it's the best thing ever, and that makes me smile.

After breakfast, Charlie asks to draw pictures at the table while I watch TV with the volume super low. This is pretty much what we do all weekend, especially since it's still cold outside. If it was warmer, I could take Charlie to the park that we always pass on the way back from the library.

Charlie's a decent artist for four years old, I guess. She thinks it's funny to draw me as a humongous head with lines coming from it for arms and legs. She sometimes stays in the lines of her coloring books, and she usually draws stuff like flowers and stars, always in pink. Today's picture is different, though. Charlie's learning her letters, and she wrote a bunch of them on her paper. It's not the neatest writing, but I can see that she's spelled out the name of Mama's drink, the name that's on all the labels. When Charlie hands me that paper and moves on to draw a pointy butterfly, I take it and put it right by Mama's bed so she'll see it when she wakes up.

March 14

"HEY, ISAIAH *DUMB*!" Angel Atkins says as soon as I sit down at our table. I ignore her like I usually do, but she's just getting started. She makes a big deal out of holding her nose and waving a hand in front of her scrunched-up face.

"Ooooh, something *stanks,* and I think it's you!" she says.

My stomach gets tight, but I just stare at the table.

"Isaiah Dumb thinks smoking is fun!" Angel laughs. I ball up my fists.

"Shut up," I say, low enough so our teacher, Mrs. Fisher, doesn't hear.

"Make me!" Angel sings, sticking out her tongue and crossing her eyes. I start thinking about ways I would make her shut up. If I was a real superhero, I'd have a pocket-sized magic vacuum that would suck up Angel's words whenever she opens her mouth. That would be cool! Maybe I'll write a poem about it in my notebook. Isaiah Dunn, the Word-Snatcher.

"Why you smilin'?" Angel demands loudly. "Must be thinking about a shower or somethin'!"

"Angel, I need you to settle down," Mrs. Fisher says. "You are talking way too much, especially when you're supposed to be working on the Morning Minute."

Angel rolls her eyes but shuts her mouth. I grin, mostly inside.

I open my workbook and read our Morning Minute assignment. Every day, Mrs. Fisher writes a sentence on the board, and we have sixty seconds to write something about it. Today, she wrote, *My world is a good and happy place.*

We're not supposed to think; just write whatever comes to our mind first. But I do think. About how the world can be good and happy for one person, but bad and sad for somebody else. And how everything can change in just one minute, one walk down the street, like it did for me, Mama, Daddy, and Charlie.

For the first time, I don't write anything. Mrs. Fisher will probably trip, but I don't know what to put down. I mean, I guess there are some happy things in my life, like Sneaky, and Daddy's notebook, and Charlie (sometimes), and Mama's good days. I really want to write a poem about all that, but right when I start to, my pencil freezes, and my page stays blank.

"Ooooh, you gonna get a big, fat zero!" whispers Angel, leaning over and looking at my workbook.

I slam the workbook shut.

"So what?" I say. "Nobody cares about that stupid Morning Minute!"

"Isaiah!" Mrs. Fisher's staring right at me, and I know she heard what I said. Angel snickers and pretends she's working hard on her assignment.

"Why don't you pull your chair up here to the front by me," Mrs. Fisher says. "Maybe that will help you get your Morning Minute finished."

I got in trouble for back-talking Mrs. Fisher last month, so I don't tell her that what would *really* help me get my Morning Minute finished is if she moves me away from Angel. She's gotta know that Angel's been messing with me all year, for no reason!

"*Now,* Isaiah," Mrs. Fisher says, with a little bit of mean in her voice, "you're holding up the class."

I want to tell her that I'm not holding up the class, because announcements just came on, and everyone's watching Gabriella Cruz and Aiden Olsen talk about the weather and today's lunch menu and spring sports. Instead, I drag my chair right next to Mrs. Fisher's messy desk without saying a word. I keep my workbook closed, too, cuz there's no way I'm writing any words about being safe and happy.

March 16

EVERYBODY SAYS SNEAKY'S gonna be a businessman when he grows up, probably cuz he has his own business right now. He sells candy at school, mainly at lunch, which is the only time I see him.

"So what you want, man? Snickers? M&M's?" he asks me once I'm halfway done with my pizza. Sneaky gets the school lunch, but he also carries a lunch pack with him, which is always stuffed with candy. Guess no one pays attention to that.

"I don't have no money," I tell him.

"You don't have a dollar?" Sneaky asks. I shake my head. "Fifty cents?"

I shake my head again. There's nothing in my pockets but lint and some rubber bands that we were using during science.

Sneaky shrugs. "Aight, man, I'll hook you up for free. Get something before I sell out."

I grin and grab a Snickers. That's why Sneaky's my boy. He always has my back.

"Yo, Sneaky, lemme get some M&M's!" calls Aiden as he walks up to our table.

"Dag, man! Chill with the loudness!" Sneaky says, looking around for the lunch monitors. He got busted for selling candy before, but that was when he tried to do it in class. Usually there's so much going on in the cafeteria that the adults haven't noticed Sneaky's operation.

Sneaky opens his lunch pack, pulls out the M&M's, and waits for Aiden to hand him a dollar, which is what he charges for most of the candy he sells. Sneaky loves dollars. But sometimes he'll only charge fifty cents if he really likes the person.

Aiden hands Sneaky a crumpled dollar and takes his candy. Sneaky slides the dollar into his pocket and is about to close his lunch pack when Aliya Morris comes up and buys two Snickers *and* a Butterfinger. I start grinning, but Sneaky gives me a look, so I don't say nothing. He's got this crush on Aliya and it's pretty pathetic. She got braces over Christmas break, and he actually thinks they make her look cuter. Weird.

My Snickers bar says something about winning a million dollars, so I read the back label to see what the rules are, imagining that my candy bar is a winner. I'm so busy thinking about what I'd do with the million dollars that I don't notice Angel marching over to our table.

"I want Skittles," she says loudly, putting a dollar on the table. I wish Sneaky would charge her two dollars!

Sneaky hands her the Skittles and gets the dollar, but when Angel starts to sit down, Sneaky shakes his head.

"Uh-uh, keep it moving," he says. "This is a jerk-free zone."

Angel narrows her eyes. "Nobody wants to sit with you anyway, Sneaky! *You* the jerk."

Sneaky ignores Angel, and she storms away. For a second, I feel bad for her. But then I remember how mean she is, and I'm glad she's gone.

"So does Sneaky make you pay, or do you get stuff for free cuz y'all are friends?" Aliya asks me.

"C'mon, girl, you can't be all up in our business like that," Sneaky says. He gets some M&M's for himself and pours a bunch in his mouth.

"Whatever," Aliya laughs.

"Don't hate the hustle," Sneaky says, zipping up his pack as the warning bell rings. "Without me, y'all would be chomping on carrot sticks all day."

He's right. This year, our school got all healthy and took out the snack machines. And at lunch, they serve Jell-O and yogurt parfaits instead of cake and cookies. We're part of some kind of pilot program that tortures kids by taking away sugar. I mean, I know it's better to eat fruits and veggies, but I sure do miss the ice cream cups we used to get.

At first, Sneaky complained just like the rest of us. Then one day he snuck in a Snickers bar for lunch, and this kid practically begged him for it. He ended up paying Sneaky two whole dollars for that Snickers. So that's when Sneaky started his candy hustle.

The bell rings, and we dump our trays and head to the playground. On our way from the cafeteria, I see a lunch monitor reach down and pick up a candy wrapper that someone dropped on the floor. The monitor frowns and asks another monitor, "Where'd this come from?" They both start scanning the kids as we rush for the door, and I nudge Sneaky.

"Yo, they're looking for candy," I whisper. Sneaky crams his lunch pack under his arm and we get out of there fast!

I'm guessing Sneaky'll think twice about selling candy at school, but it's the complete opposite!

"I gotta sell four more candy bars," he tells me once we're on the playground by the monkey bars. "Then I'll be halfway there."

Sneaky got his nickname because he was always sneaking something when he was little, but now that he's older, the nickname sticks because he's also into sneakers, especially Jordans. He's saving for a new pair now, and he'll probably have them in no time. I like shoes, too, but if I had a hustle, all my money would go toward getting us out of Smoky Inn.

March 21

THE *ONE* GOOD thing about Mama being tired all the time is that I get to go to the library almost every day. It takes about fifteen minutes to walk there from my school, and I stay until Mama picks me up, usually when it's closing. At first I was mad that Mama stopped picking me up right after school. Now I'm glad I have a cool place to go, with no stinky smoke smells.

"Hey, Mr. Shephard," I say, giving my favorite librarian a fist bump. "Have you heard about the contest yet?"

Mr. Shephard chuckles.

"Isaiah Dunn, King of Questions," he says. "They announce the winners on April seventeenth, remember?"

I sigh. "I know, but I thought maybe you already knew."

"Nope!" Mr. Shephard grabs a stack of books from a table and takes them to a cart. "I'm not one of the judges this year."

I sit down at my favorite table by the window and pull out Daddy's notebook. I entered one of his stories in the library's short-story contest, and I can't wait to find out if he won. The $300 prize money would definitely help us get out of Smoky Inn.

"You're flying through that, aren't you?" Mr. Shephard nods toward the notebook.

"Yeah," I say. Only fifty-one pages left now.

Mr. Shephard raises an eyebrow. "Usually kids are super excited when they get close to the end. What's up?"

I shrug, not knowing how to tell him that once I'm done with this notebook, I'm done with Daddy's words.

Mr. Shephard thinks for a second.

"I get it, man," he says. "If what you're reading is really good, you never want it to end, right?"

"Yeah," I say.

"Well, here's a trick," Mr. Shephard continues. "Don't think of it as an ending; just a pause button till you read the next great thing."

"Pause button?"

Mr. Shephard nods. "That's your dad's notebook, right? So when you finish that one, see if he'll let you read another one. Trust me, a true writer never has just one notebook. Plus, you could always just read that one all over again."

Mr. Shephard pats me on the back and goes off to put the books away.

In the story I'm reading, Isaiah Dunn just got pulled out of class by secret agents, who tell him he needs to go undercover at a championship basketball game to expose a corrupt principal. I feel like *my* secret mission is to find out where Daddy's notebooks are, so I bombard Mama as soon as I climb into the car.

"Mama, did Daddy have other notebooks?"

"Well, hello to you, too," Mama says, looking at me in the rearview mirror.

"Yeah, hello to you, too!" Charlie echoes around the two fingers she has in her mouth.

"How was school?" Mama asks, making sure I buckle up before she starts driving.

"Good," I say, "but, Mama, did Daddy have other notebooks?"

Mama stops at a light, and her eyes find mine in the rearview again.

"You didn't say hi to me, 'Saiah." Charlie pouts.

"Hi, okay?" I tell her. "And take your fingers out your mouth!"

I lean forward, closer to Mama's ear, even though I know she heard me. I don't want to bug her, but this is important!

"Mama, are there—"

"I heard you, Isaiah," Mama says. Her tone's not mad or anything, but she's taking forever to answer. I tap my foot, like maybe that'll speed her up.

I stare at a homeless guy crossing the street, hunched down and slow, and it makes me even more impatient.

"Mr. Shephard says all writers have more than one notebook," I tell her. "So I bet Daddy had tons of them, right?"

"Yes," Mama says finally, so softly I don't even hear her at first.

"Where are they? You still have them, right?" I'm leaning forward again, too close to Mama's ear.

"Sit back," Mama says, and this time her voice is much more serious. "I got other things to worry about than finding some old notebooks."

"But, Mama, I'm almost done with—"

Mama slams on the brakes, and me and Charlie lurch forward. A driver behind us blares on his horn and swerves around.

"Isaiah, do NOT ask me again!" Mama says. I'm gripping my seat belt super tight when Mama starts driving again.

"Why did you do that, Mama?" Charlie asks. Mama doesn't answer.

I see the stupid motel sign up ahead, and my stomach clenches up even more.

"We're home!" Charlie calls, pointing a spitty finger at the window.

I hit her on the arm.

"Charlie, that ain't our house," I say sternly. "We're just staying there for a little while."

Charlie rubs her arm, but doesn't scream "Owwww!" like she usually does.

March 25

MAMA HAS GOOD days and bad days, and I never know which one it's gonna be. Like today, she's awake before me and Charlie, but she's just sitting up in bed staring at nothing, so I think it's gonna be a bad one.

"Mama, you okay?" I ask with a groggy voice.

Mama looks at me, and she smiles.

"Of course, baby," she says. Then she goes left field. "One day, baby, you gonna wake up, and your voice will be as deep as your daddy's!"

She's laughing, so I do my deepest deep-voice impression.

"What'cho mean, one day? It's already deep!"

"All right, li'l Barry White," Mama says. She moves her covers and nudges Charlie, who's curled up in a ball. "Wake up, Sleeping Beauty. We got somewhere to be."

"Where we going, Mama?" I ask. But it doesn't really matter to me, as long as we get to leave this room.

"I have some tickets to the children's museum, and they expire tomorrow."

"For real?"

I've only been to the children's museum a couple of times, and both times Daddy was there. I watch Mama's face for sad shadows, but she seems okay.

"Yes, for real," she says. She walks to the tiny kitchen area and gets bowls for cereal. She actually starts to sing!

"Charlie baby, Charlie baby, get on up! Charlie baby, Charlie baby, strut yo' stuff!"

I can't stop my eyes from getting big, cuz Mama hasn't sung in forever! I bounce on her and Charlie's bed until Charlie starts to whine.

"'Saiah, I'm sleepin'!" she says, all attitude-y.

"It's time to get up, Charlie baby!" I tell her, real close to her ear the way she does to me.

"Stop!" she says. Whew! That morning breath ain't no joke! I back up and fan the air in front of my face.

"Yeesh! You need to go brush your teeth!" I say. I dig through my green basket of clothes until I find my black jeans with no holes. I put on one of my nice shirts, the kind with buttons, and go to the bathroom to brush my teeth and wash my face. I can still hear Mama humming the Charlie song, and I pray real hard that the *whole* day is just like right now—happy. I tell God that I'll do everything I can to make sure Charlie behaves, but He'll have to handle Mama. That's only fair.

We take the bus to the museum, "for the experience," Mama says. I get my own seat for most of the ride, but an old man slides next to me once we're almost there.

"Is that the museum, Mama?" asks Charlie from the seat across from me.

"No, baby, that's the hospital," Mama says.

My heart beats a little faster, and I'm afraid to look at Mama. Was this the hospital they took Daddy to? Mama's face still has a smile on it, and she wraps an arm around Charlie and pulls her close. I relax a little and turn back to the window. A few minutes later, Charlie's at it again.

"Mama, is *that* the museum?"

"Charlie, stop!" I hiss, nudging her pink sneaker with my foot. Mama looks out the window and pats Charlie's leg.

"Charlie, that's a church!" Mama says, giving Charlie a tickle. "You know that!"

Charlie giggles and settles into Mama, and for a quick second, I wish it was me sitting there, close to Mama, laughing. Or even better, I wish that it was Daddy sitting next to me instead of the old man who keeps bumping me with his arm.

Charlie turns it into a game after that. She's all, "Mama, is that the museum?" when we pass a car wash, and, "What about that, Mama?" when we stop at a light in front of a real fancy restaurant. Mama plays along, and I want Charlie to stop so bad! I don't want Mama to use up all her happy before we even get there.

Finally, Mama says, "This is us," pushes a button, and a few minutes later, we're inside the museum. We stand in a line that's kinda long, and when we finally get to the front, Mama hands the clerk our tickets. One thing I notice, though, is that Mama really has *four* tickets. She puts one back into her purse super fast, and I pretend not to see.

Daddy's ticket. Now I remember him telling us that we'd go to the museum over Christmas break. I can't help but feel down for a second, cuz he's not here, but I'm also glad *we* are.

"Enjoy your time," says the ticket clerk with a huge smile.

"Thank you, we sure will," Mama replies, and she has a big smile, too. Whew!

Inside the museum, me and Charlie make huge bubbles, create a song on a giant keyboard, and pedal a bike that makes a light come on. Even Mama has fun with that, and we talk about riding our bikes once it's summer.

Before we leave, Mama gets us pretzels and pop in the museum snack shop. She doesn't get a pretzel for herself, but she takes a bite out of mine and Charlie's.

"Not bad," she says.

"Why don't you get another one, Mama?" I ask.

"Nah." Mama shakes her head and smiles. "Mama's not that hungry."

I shrug and take another bite of the warm, salty pretzel, thinking that this is the best day in forever.

"Look at that, Charlie," I say, pointing to the girl twisting dough into the shape of a pretzel. She moves her hands so fast, it's like magic.

"I wanna get a job doing that," I say. Mama smiles.

"You have five, six years before you have to worry about getting a job," she says.

But she's wrong. I'm worrying about getting a job right now.

We watch the pretzel girl a little longer, but then Mama looks at her watch, taps the table, and tells us we gotta catch the bus back. Charlie can't finish her pretzel, so Mama gobbles it up. I guess she was hungry after all.

It's colder when we go outside, and the sun is setting, but we're all happy anyway. I grab one of Charlie's hands, and Mama grabs the other, and we stand outside the museum. Once we're back on the bus, I stare out the window at the buildings and cars, and especially the people. I think about how I can see all of them, but they can't see me; and even if they can, they still don't *know* me. They have no clue that me and Mama and Charlie had the most awesome day ever, or that we need a ton more.

I can't get out a poem when I try to write in my notebook later, but at least I have a few words to add. *Happy. warm. sunset. safe.*

March 30

"HEY, MAMA, THE hot water's not working!" I say, peeking my head out of the bathroom door. Mama and Charlie are in their bed—Charlie asleep, and Mama staring at the old detective show on TV. She doesn't even look my way. I see a bottle on the raggedy nightstand by her side of the bed. She doesn't even rip the labels off anymore, like she used to.

"Mama," I say again. "I'm trying to take my shower but the—"

"What am I supposed to do, Isaiah?" she snaps. "Go to the office and tell them!"

I close the bathroom door and turn off the freezing cold water. I was letting it run, thinking maybe it would change to hot, but it was still ice after five minutes. I pull my jeans and T-shirt back on and open the door again, kinda hoping that maybe Mama went down to the office herself.

Nope. She's still in the bed, watching—but not *really* watching—the TV. She does the same thing with me and Charlie—watching us but not *really* watching.

I zip up my jacket and make sure my key card is in the pocket where I always keep it. I walk outside into the cold, dark night and follow the sidewalk to the office. When I open the door, I feel like coughing. Man, why does everywhere smell like smoke around here? The guy at the desk nods at me but doesn't say anything.

"Hey, we're in 109 and the hot water isn't working."

The guy looks at a sheet in front of him, and then up at me, his face all funky.

"Room 109?" he asks. "You're lucky you got water at all. You're two weeks late."

"Late for what?" I ask him, frowning.

"Paying for the room," the guy says, like, duh! "Money's due on Friday. *Every* Friday. Tell your mother that."

I just stare at him. How am I supposed to know about the money for the room? I've seen Mama bring cash to the office before, lots of times. Maybe she forgot?

The guy shakes his head, like maybe he's remembering that I'm just a kid. Then he sighs, like I just disturbed his amazing life by walking in.

"Well, all right," he says, shooing me off with his words when someone else walks in. "We'll send somebody to look at it."

I walk past the man and lady who just came in and jog back to 109. I always call it that—109. It's not our room; it's not our home. It's just 109.

"They said they'll send somebody," I tell Mama. "They also said they need money for the room."

Mama doesn't say a word. She barely blinks, but when she does, it's super slow, like her eyelids are exhausted.

I was gonna do my math homework after my shower, but

now I just yank out the sofa bed and climb under the covers without taking my clothes off, remembering how Mama used to yell at me for doing that.

April 3

I GET A bad feeling the second Mrs. Fisher says, "Class, today marks the third day of National Poetry Month, and we're going to form groups of two for our poetry unit." I look around the room, wondering who I'll pick to be my partner. Maybe Kevon or Malik. But then Mrs. Fisher flips it.

"I have each of your names in this tin, and I'll pull two names at a time. The two names I pick will be partners."

The class groans, including me. Everyone wants to just pick their own partner, but Mrs. Fisher tells us we'll actually be more productive by working with a partner she chooses. Nobody buys it. Mrs. Fisher starts reading names, and I hold my breath.

"Greg and Malik. Frankie and Marissa. A.J. and Zoe. Kira and Amani. Kevon and Staci."

This is not looking good. My stomach is going crazy, and I squeeze my pencil so tight, I could break it.

"Isaiah and Angel."

My head drops. This has to be a late April Fools' joke!

"Uh-uh, Miz Fisher, no!" Angel says loudly, shaking her head so hard, the beads on her braids make clicking sounds. "I'm not working with him."

Mrs. Fisher pauses, and for a second, I think she's gonna draw a new name for Angel. Nope!

"Angel, that's unnecessary. I'm sure you and Isaiah will work fine together."

"No, we won't," Angel says in a rude whisper. Mrs. Fisher's already calling the rest of the names, so she doesn't hear.

I have the worst luck in the history of luck. Not only do I have to sit by Angel every day, but now she's my partner. Mrs. Fisher says we'll have fifteen minutes every day to work on our project together, and we'll present at the end of the month. Great. Fifteen minutes of torture.

The thing is, this should be my favorite month of the year, where everything is about poems, and I can just write and write and write. But all I do is sit frozen when Mrs. Fisher reads us a poem about baseball and asks us to write one of our own.

"Why I gotta get stuck with Isaiah Dumb?" Angel says when we move our chairs closer for partner time. "Do you even know how to write anything?"

"I can write way better than you," I tell her.

"Prove it," Angel says. "Write a poem right now."

My stomach churns like a blender. Man, if this was last year,

I could do it easy. But since November 24, my words just won't come. Angel's sticking her lips out and glaring at me, and I know my words will never make it to the paper in front of me.

"I'm not writing nothing," I tell Angel. She laughs.

"See? Isaiah Dumb; betcha can't even read!"

The cuss word's outta my mouth before I can stop it, and everyone at my table goes "Oooooh!" Angel tells Mrs. Fisher what I said, and Mrs. Fisher tells me to go to the office.

"She keeps calling me Isaiah Dumb!" I tell Mrs. Fisher. No way should I get in trouble and not Angel.

"Angel, is that true?" asks Mrs. Fisher.

"No," says Angel, with a smirk on her face. "I'm saying his last name, *Dunn*. Maybe he can't hear good."

"Isaiah, go speak with Mr. Tobin. You know we do not speak that way in this classroom."

Angel smiles and waves at me on my way out, and I clench my fists to keep from throwing something right at her head. I imagine using a superpower to send her to the principal's office instead of me. Even better, maybe I'd just send her to a different country, a different continent. Somewhere in Antarctica, with penguins who smack her in the face when she talks. I think about this the whole time I'm walking down the hall to Mr. Tobin's office, and I feel a tiny bit better when I get there.

"Hello, Isaiah, what brings you down to the office?" asks Ms. Kenney, the secretary.

"I cussed in class," I tell Ms. Kenney.

"Oh no, that's not good at all," Ms. Kenney says, some of the niceness leaving her face. "Why don't you have a seat and wait for Mr. Tobin. He's finishing up with someone right now."

I sit down and wonder how Ms. Kenney knows Mr. Tobin is finishing up. His door is closed. He's probably in there talking to some kid about respect and kindness, just like he told me when I got in trouble for telling Mrs. Fisher that her breath stank.

I listen to Ms. Kenney type and wonder what kind of story Daddy would write about her. Maybe she's an undercover spy who taps a Morse code message to the superhero Isaiah Dunn. *Click, click,* pause, *click, click, click.* Maybe that means "get out now, danger ahead!"

I stare at the rocket clock in the office, and the second hand has stars on it that go around and around. Our school mascot is a rocket, and right about now I'm wishing I could shoot off into space instead of waiting for Mr. Tobin. I also wish I had Daddy's notebook to pass the time.

After forever, Mr. Tobin's door opens, and two kids come out looking mad. Mr. Tobin tells Ms. Kenney to call their parents, and I know that means they're suspended. Gulp.

"Isaiah, why are you in my office again?" Mr. Tobin's voice booms, and I jump a little.

"I said a cuss word in class," I say, staring at my shoes.

Mr. Tobin's tone doesn't change. "Come on in."

This is only my third time in Mr. Tobin's office, and I bet he doesn't even remember the first time. That was two years ago, in third grade, when me and Sneaky snuck into the cafeteria to get extra chocolate milk cartons.

"Why were you cursing in class, Isaiah?" asks Mr. Tobin once we sit down.

"I don't know."

Mr. Tobin smiles. "I think what you do know is that I need real answers when you're in here, not 'I don't know.'"

I can tell Mr. Tobin wants me to say something, but I don't.

"So, I'll ask again. Why were you cursing in class?"

"I only said one word."

"And why did you say that word?"

I shrug, and Mr. Tobin shakes his head.

"Because somebody called me dumb."

"Who called you dumb?" asks Mr. Tobin.

"Somebody in my class."

Mr. Tobin sighs. "So someone called you a name, and you called them one back."

I shrug again.

"Is someone bullying you, Isaiah?" asks Mr. Tobin.

"No," I say. Angel's annoying and mean, but it's not like she's beating me up or stealing my stuff. That's what Curtis Wilson did to kids last year, and he got kicked out of school.

"If you were upset that someone called you a name, why didn't you tell your teacher?"

"Miz Fisher ain't gonna do nothing," I say.

"Why do you think that?" Mr. Tobin asks.

"Cuz she never does. I'm the only one who gets in trouble."

Mr. Tobin thinks about that for a second.

"I understand it might feel that way sometimes, but in the future, we really need for you to say something if a classmate is bothering you. Don't try to handle it all yourself, okay?"

I nod, but I already know Mr. Tobin's way doesn't work.

"Also, I'd like for you to spend an hour in the Reflection Room with Ms. Marlee before returning to class," Mr. Tobin says.

I slouch in my chair and groan. Ms. Marlee is one of the school counselors, and the Reflection Room is where you go to think about what you did. They made me see Ms. Marlee after Daddy died. She's okay and all, but I don't feel like talking right now.

"Is there a problem?" Mr. Tobin asks. He has a stern look on his face, so I shake my head no.

"Good. I really hope this is the last time I see you in here, Isaiah," Mr. Tobin says, writing my pass to the Reflection Room. "At least, for anything negative. School should be safe and fun, and it's up to you to let us know when something is wrong."

"Okay," I tell him. He said the exact same thing last time, so I do, too. But I know that even if I did tell Mrs. Fisher and Mr. Tobin, nothing is gonna stop Angel from being how she is.

April 4

TODAY, MAMA PICKS me up early from the library and we drive to Sudz-O-Rama to wash clothes. I love the way Sudz-O-Rama smells, clean and bubbly. Our clothes always start out that way, too, but once we take them back to 109, the smoke smell grabs them and holds on tight.

"Mama, how long we gotta be at the Smoky Inn?" I ask.

"What?" Mama raises an eyebrow.

"The motel," I say. I didn't mean to say what I call the place. "How much longer do we have to be there?"

Mama's folding up all the white clothes, and Charlie's hypnotized watching the color clothes go round and round in the washer. Can't blame her, I guess. It's kinda cool to watch the blues and pinks and yellows swirl around and get soapy.

"I don't know, Isaiah," Mama answers. "But we won't be there forever." Her saying that makes me feel better, even though I wish she'd say we're moving back to our place tomorrow. We'll be out of Smoky Inn in no time if Daddy's story wins the contest. Waiting is so hard!

"I'm getting some things together," Mama continues, putting my T-shirts and socks in my green basket. "And we're gonna have a really nice place this time."

"With a playroom, Mama?" Charlie asks, still watching the clothes.

"Yeah, with a playroom," Mama tells her. Then she laughs, "Shoot, maybe two playrooms! Isaiah, what do you want our new place to have?"

"Two bathrooms," I say. "No, three."

Mama laughs some more, and she's probably thinking the same thing I am. Our old apartment only had one bathroom, and once I had to go #2 really, really bad, but Daddy was doing the same thing. So Mama told me to use Charlie's princess potty. I said no way, but the longer Daddy took, the more I had to go. So I used it. They called me Princess Poopy for a long time after that.

"Two bathrooms for sure," Mama says, "and a room for my plants."

"When are we moving?" Charlie asks.

"Soon."

Soon can mean a lot of things, and just when I'm about to ask Mama how soon, she hands me two dollars and tells me to get something from the vending machine for me and Charlie.

"C'mon," I tell Charlie, grabbing her arm. She pulls her arm away, and I hate when she does that.

At the machine, she puts her face super close to the glass.

"I want Cheetos, Isaiah," she says, pointing. "It says B One Two."

"Those gonna make your hands all nasty," I tell her.

"So?"

"So you should get the animal crackers or something."

"I don't want animal crackers," Charlie says. "I want Cheetos!"

"Okay, whatever." I put in the dollar and get her the Cheetos. Of course, the first thing she does is ask me to open them for her. I open the bag and swipe two Cheetos before handing it to her.

"He-ey!" Charlie yells, and the lady loading her clothes into a dryer near us looks over with a frown.

"Charlie, shhh!" I say. Charlie scrunches up her eyebrows and crosses her arms super hard, and she almost spills her Cheetos.

"Stop all that," I tell her. "It ain't cute."

I turn back to the vending machine and decide on the strawberry frosted Pop-Tarts, mostly cuz there's two in the pack. I walk back over to Mama and Charlie, who glares at me and then crunches on a Cheeto.

"Mama, want a Pop-Tart?"

"No, thank you, baby."

I sit by Charlie and hand her a piece of my Pop-Tart before she can even beg me, and she shoves it into her mouth. She tells me "thank you," and I don't even yell at her when she puts her sticky Cheeto hand on my jeans. That's cuz I hear Mama say something real softly.

"Gary."

It's Daddy's name. When I look closer, I see what made Mama say it. She's holding one of Daddy's socks, a long one with the word *Hanes* where his toes go. She's holding the sock and crying softly, right in the middle of the Laundromat, and I have no idea what to do. It's probably the match to the sock I use to store my cash. My throat gets tight, and I can barely swallow the Pop-Tart.

"I'm thirsty."

Charlie tugging on my sleeve unfreezes my brain.

"C'mon," I tell her, and we walk back over to the vending machine, even though I know we don't have enough for anything.

"How 'bout that one, 'Saiah?" Charlie asks, pointing to the orange Crush. I touch the quarter in my pocket.

"We don't have enough."

"Okay, that one!" Charlie points to the 7UP, and it's the exact same price.

"It costs the same, Charlie," I say. "Let's just find a water fountain."

Charlie digs in her pocket and pulls out two quarters.

"Is this enough, 'Saiah?"

"Where'd you get that?"

"I found it," Charlie says, bouncing up and down. Before I can stop her, she puts the quarters in.

"We still don't have enough, Charlie!" I say, going to push the button to get our money back. "We need one more quarter."

"Here y'all go."

I turn around and see the lady who was loading her dryer earlier. She holds out a quarter.

"You say you just need a quarter? I got an extra one."

"Thank you!" Charlie squeals, plucking the quarter from the lady's hand and putting it into the slot. I have no choice but to take the quarter from my pocket and feed it to the machine. I push A13 for the Crush.

"Thanks," I say to the lady, who smiles and nods.

I peek over at Mama, and she seems okay now. I feel like I would be okay, too, if I could just take the words swirling around in my head and smoosh them into a poem in my notebook. *Stuck. Alone. Scared. Little. Daddy, what do I do?*

"Isaiah, help me carry these baskets," Mama says. I push the words away and do what she says.

I look around, but I don't see Daddy's sock anywhere. It's just like him.

Gone.

April 7

"DO YOU LIKE it here, 'Saiah?" asks Charlie. We're both on my sofa bed in 109, watching TV and waiting for Mama to get home.

"No," I tell Charlie. "I hate it."

"Does Mama like it?"

I shrug. I don't know if Mama likes anything as much as her bottles, which I'm starting to see more and more, but I don't tell Charlie that.

"Mama should get us a new house," Charlie says, moving a little closer to me. Normally, I would push her away, but tonight I just let her stay close.

"She will," I say. "Soon."

Charlie sighs, like "yeah, yeah, I heard that before."

"Charlie"—I turn the TV down and look at my little sister— "I'm gonna help Mama, you know. I'm saving my money, and we're gonna have the best house ever."

"For real?" Charlie's eyes get big and excited, and I know she believes me.

"Yeah."

"Can you turn it up now?" Charlie points at the TV.

"Yeah."

Me and Charlie watch TV till we're both starving. I open the mini-fridge, and there's not much inside. I warm up bowls of beans and rice, which we already had two days in a row. I tell

Charlie that in Daddy's stories, the beans and rice have magical powers, and she eats it without whining.

"Can you read it to me, Isaiah?" she asks, scraping up her last bite. I'm nowhere near done, cuz I'm super sick of beans and rice. Maybe I can find a recipe for something else and surprise Mama. I'm thinking about what I'll make when Charlie bangs her spoon against the bowl to get my attention. Annoying.

"Isaiah, I said, can you read it to me?"

"Read what? Daddy's stories?"

Charlie nods.

"I guess," I say. We leave our bowls on the table and climb onto the sofa bed. I don't even make Charlie brush her teeth or put on her pajamas first.

I grab the gold notebook and read her the story of Isaiah Dunn having to stop a train from ramming into a building. Charlie's so close, I can smell her bean breath, but I don't clown her for it.

"Daddy writed a good story," Charlie says through a yawn.

"*Wrote* a good story," I say, correcting her.

"Yeah," she says. "Isaiah Dunn is my hero."

Charlie asks if she can sleep in my bed, and I say yeah. Soon she starts breathing heavy, and I know she's knocked out, but I stay up a long time thinking about what she said, about Isaiah Dunn being her hero. I wish she was talking about *me*, not some made-up kid in a story.

April 8

"ISAIAH, CHARLIE, GET your shoes on, we're going to the store," Mama tells us. *It's about time,* I think, but I don't say that out loud. I'm just glad she's up and dressed.

In the car, Mama hums a little to the radio, which is good. Right after Daddy died, she would cry to almost every song that came on, and I wished she would just keep the radio off. I cross my fingers and hope that no sad songs come on.

Soon we pull up to a building, but it's not Walmart. The sign out front says "Seven Baskets," and it looks more like a church than a store.

"What is this, Mama?" I ask, scrunching up my face.

"The store," she says, taking Charlie's hand and heading for the entrance. I follow her, but something doesn't feel right.

Inside, a lady in a green shirt walks right up to us, all smiling and happy.

"Welcome to Seven Baskets!" the lady says. "My name is Joy, and I'll be helping you shop today." I make a face. Helping us shop? That's pretty weird. The Joy lady asks Mama if she had an appointment time, and since Mama doesn't, we have to sit down and wait for a little bit.

"What kind of store is this, Mama?" I ask, looking around at the aisles. There's a mom with two daughters pushing a cart around, and a guy and a girl with one, too. Both have helpers with them who are wearing the same green shirts as Joy.

"It's a store where we can get groceries," says Mama.

"But we usually get stuff at Walmart."

"Well, today we're getting our things here," Mama tells me.

I don't know why, but being here bothers me. Before I can ask Mama any more questions, Joy bounces over to us.

"Okay, Lisa, we're all ready for you guys. Go ahead and grab a cart and we'll get started."

We follow Joy to the first aisle of groceries, and she starts explaining how things work.

"So as we go down each aisle, I'll tell you what your family can purchase from each food group." Joy points to the row of cans in front of us. "You guys are a family of three, so you can grab three cans, plus a bag of dry beans."

And that's how it goes. We roll up and down the aisles, and Joy tells us what we can pick.

"Ewww! Mama, I want Froot Loops!" Charlie makes a face when Mama puts a box of Cheerios into our cart, only they're not the *real* Cheerios, they're Honey Spins, and they have a scary-looking bee on the front. The bee looks like it ate too much of Sneaky's candy. I don't say anything about wishing for Frosted Flakes.

"Hush, Charlie," Mama says, taking a peek at Joy, who's still smiling.

Mama picks up some oatmeal and a big bag of pancake mix. "We're out of syrup," I tell her.

Joy overhears me and looks around. "Oh, I'm sorry, buddy, I'm not sure we received any syrup today. But I'll check with Ralph in the back."

In the next aisle, Mama goes for the biggest bag of rice I've ever seen, and I imagine her cooking me magic beans and rice, like in Daddy's stories.

We put the healthy kind of bread in our cart, plus milk, juice, some frozen pieces of chicken, and a bag of potatoes that have brown spots on them. We go through a checkout line where Joy writes some things down, but I don't see Mama pay anything.

What I *do* see, though, makes me want to disappear into thin air. Right as Joy says, "Thanks for coming; we'll see you next month," I lock eyes with Angel Atkins, who's walking into Seven Baskets with her mom and brothers and sisters. She stares at me and I stare at her; my heart's probably thumping hard enough to make my shirt move. Just great! Angel's the last person I want to see in a place like this. I can tell she's here to shop with her family, too, but the way she smirks and rolls her eyes lets me know that things are gonna be even worse with me and her.

"Isaiah? You gonna push the cart for me?" Mama asks, forcing me to turn away from Angel. I grab the cart and push so hard, I run into a basket of lotions and soaps. I don't turn around to look, but I'm sure Angel's watching, laughing her head off. I keep telling myself she won't be laughing for long. I'm gonna make so much money, we'll move to a house in a whole different city, and I'll go to a new school and never have to see Angel Atkins again.

April 10

"OOOH, YOU STINK!" says Angel, making a face the minute I sit down.

"Yeah, just like your mama," I say back. I'm so sick of her messin' with me!

"Oooh, burn!" laughs Kevon.

"At least my mama don't make me wear the same clothes every day!" Angel says, glaring at me like "Gotcha!" I freeze for a second, wondering if she knows. How could she know? Kevon's head swivels to me, waiting for me to put the smack down on Angel.

I open my mouth, not sure what's gonna come out, but Mrs. Fisher cuts me off.

"Isaiah, no talking during announcements," she says with a frown.

"Yeah, your breath is distracting me," Angel says.

"Your ugly face is a distraction!" I tell her. She just doesn't know how close I am to exploding.

"Isaiah! I said be quiet!" Mrs. Fisher stands up. "Have you completed your Morning Minute?"

"No."

"Well, focus on that instead of talking."

I roll my eyes. I wanna tell Mrs. Fisher there's no way I'm writing about "my favorite room in my house" when I have no house. I open Daddy's notebook instead and read a story about a little girl seeing the ocean for the first time. The little girl sounds a lot like Charlie.

"What's that?" whispers Kevon.

"None of your business."

Kevon frowns and keeps working on his Morning Minute. I'm not trying to be mean, but Kevon's not Sneaky, and this stuff is personal.

The announcements go off, and Mrs. Fisher starts talking about our language arts project, but I don't stop reading. I want Daddy's words to magically sweep me away from here, like the waves he wrote about.

"Isaiah, bring that up here, please."

Mrs. Fisher's voice is like a Mama-smack on the back of the head, and I jump.

"Bring what up where?" I ask, putting my hand on top of the notebook. Eyes glue themselves on me, including Angel's.

"You know *exactly* what I'm talking about," Mrs. Fisher says. "Bring it up right now. You may have it back at the end of class."

"Maaaan!" I groan extra loud and stand up slowly. I don't like the idea of Daddy's notebook being in Mrs. Fisher's nasty spit fingers. She's one of those people who licks her fingers when she passes back papers, and I always end up with a wet thumbprint. Gross!

I grip Daddy's notebook in my hand, and I already know I'm not letting go of it.

Next thing I know, I'm tripping over something and almost face-plant in front of everyone. Kids laugh, including Angel. But her laugh is different. Mean.

"Dang, watch it, Isaiah Dumb!" she says.

That's when I snap. I narrow my eyes and shove her as hard as I can. Both her and her chair go flying backward, and then she's looking up at me with shocked eyes.

I barely hear Mrs. Fisher yell at me to get out of her class. She reaches for her classroom phone and calls for Mr. Simms, one of the safety monitors, but I don't wait for him to get there. I just take my notebook and leave. It doesn't take long for Mr. Simms to find me.

"Hey, slow it down there," Mr. Simms says. "You know our walk is gonna be to the office, right?"

I don't answer. Me and Mr. Simms walk in the same rhythm: left, right, left, right.

"So what's going on?" he asks me.

"Nothing."

When we get into the office, Mr. Tobin's standing by his door. Man, Mrs. Fisher made her phone calls pretty fast.

"Inside, Mr. Dunn," Mr. Tobin says, super serious. I follow him and sit in the same chair I always do. Mr. Tobin sits, too, and stares me down.

"I just got a disturbing call from Mrs. Fisher. Again," he says, and I can tell he's not playing this time. "Why don't you share with me what happened in her class, and why you decided to disregard what we talked about last time."

"Angel Atkins calls me names and messes with me all the time. Today she tripped me in front of everyone, so I pushed her, and she fell out her chair."

Mr. Tobin studies me for a sec, like he didn't expect me to confess everything right away.

"Isaiah," he says finally, "I think you know that we can't have this kind of behavior at school."

I don't say anything, but I'm wondering if we also can't have Angel's behavior at school.

Mr. Tobin grabs something off the bookcase behind him and holds it up.

"Remember this?" he asks. I look at what's in his hand. *Woodson Elementary Student Code of Conduct.*

I shrug.

Mr. Tobin flips through the pages and hands the booklet to me.

"I want you to read the section on fighting," he says. When I don't take the book right away, he clears his throat.

"That would be now, Isaiah."

I sigh and take the book. I stare at the page but don't read a thing. Instead, I pretend it's one of Daddy's stories, that I'm Isaiah Dunn, Superhero, cracking a code that an evil principal has hidden inside a—

"Isaiah."

"Huh?"

"You didn't answer my question. What if your classmate had gotten seriously hurt?"

"I don't know," I say, not really caring if Angel was hurt or not.

"You said she's been teasing you." Mr. Tobin waits.

"Yeah."

"Did you talk to Mrs. Fisher about this, or to Ms. Marlee when you saw her?"

"No."

"Why not?"

I shrug and study my shoes. I'm getting a hole where my big toe is. Sneaky would flip out if he found a hole in one of his shoes. I wonder what pair he's gonna buy next.

Mr. Tobin taps his fingers on his desk.

"I know you've been dealing with a lot, Isaiah," he says. "How are you and your mom doing?"

"Good."

"Anything happening at home that you need to talk about?"

I shake my head. No home, so nothing to talk about.

Mr. Tobin says that even though I'm dealing with loss, my behavior is unacceptable. He says he has to suspend me. And that he has to call Mama. That's when I start to get nervous. Mr. Tobin types on his computer and then picks up the phone. I stare at a crack near the bottom of Mr. Tobin's desk and pray mad hard that Mama's okay when she answers.

"Hello, Mrs. Dunn? This is Principal Tobin from Woodson Elementary." He pauses, and a small frown crosses his face. My stomach flips, and my palms get sweaty.

"I said, this is Mr. Tobin, principal at Woodson." A pause. Mr. Tobin taps his pen on his desk, gives me a funny look. "Well, Isaiah got into some trouble today. He'll have to serve a five-day suspension, and we'll need you to come pick him up."

That's when I hear Mama's voice through the phone, and it's not pretty. Mr. Tobin tells Mama we'll have a follow-up meeting when I come back. It's super quiet when Mr. Tobin hangs up, like a thick secret is floating around.

"Your mom wanted you to walk to the library," Mr. Tobin says.

I stand up quickly, but he's not done yet.

"But I told her she personally needs to pick you up."

"Huh?"

"Is that where you go after school?"

"Yeah."

"And your mother picks you up from there?"

"Yeah."

"Where does your mom work?"

"I don't know," I tell Mr. Tobin. I think about Mama's old job, and how she keeps telling us she's gonna try to go back. Mr. Tobin needs to stop buggin' me with all these questions!

"Okay, Isaiah, wait in the lobby with Ms. Kenney until your mom gets here."

I sit in the chair closest to the door and listen to the rocket clock ticking and Ms. Kenney typing and answering the phone with "Woodson Elementary, how can I help you?" As soon as I see Mama coming in the front door, I jump up.

"Hold on, Isaiah," Ms. Kenney says. "She'll have to sign you out."

"But—" I want to tell Ms. Kenney that's a bad idea, cuz I see Mama coming, and she doesn't look good at all. Before I can even think of a superhero move to get me away from all of this, Mama's busting into the office. Her eyes find me, and I want to disappear.

"Isaiah?" Her voice is strange and loud. "Today? You wanna act a fool today?"

I open my mouth to tell her what happened, but she shakes her head.

"No. Don't even say anything. Come on, let's go."

"Ma'am, you'll need to sign Isaiah out," Ms. Kenney says. "And I believe Mr. Tobin wants to—"

"I don't have time for all that," Mama says. She scribbles her name on the clipboard on Ms. Kenney's desk. "You called me up here to get Isaiah, so that's what I'm doing." Mama looks at me. "I said, come on!"

We move toward the door, and Mama waves off Mr. Tobin when he heads over, asking Mama to calm down and talk with him for a minute.

I keep my eyes glued to the ground all the way to the car.

April 13

SNEAKY PRETTY MUCH sucks at basketball, but he always wants to play. We're at the park near where he lives, and he's losing a game of H-O-R-S-E. It's the first time I've been away from Smoky Inn since I got suspended. Mama says it's not supposed to be all fun and games. She barely listened when I tried to tell her what happened, just shook her head and said she couldn't believe I got put out of school. I wanna tell her I'm not some bad kid, but she should already know that. So after a while, I just stop explaining.

Being suspended sucks. I always thought it would mean

playing video games in your pajamas all day and eating cereal from a huge mixing bowl. That's what Sneaky said he got to do the time he was suspended. It's a whole lot different for me. Suspended means being stuck at the Smoky Inn, watching Charlie and hoping Mama doesn't stay mad. Never thought I would miss being at school. The only reason I'm at the park now is cuz Mama brought Charlie to Miz Rita's to get her hair done.

"Okay, let's play *elephant* this time," Sneaky says after I beat him in the first game. I laugh when his shot bangs off the rim and he gets an *E* right away.

"You still gonna lose," I tell him, grabbing the ball and making a layup. Sneaky tries it, too. Gets an *L*.

"Man, shut up!" Sneaky says. "Betcha a dollar I make this shot!"

Sneaky's a little bit in front of the free-throw line, but I'm pretty sure he'll miss.

"Bet."

He shoots way too hard and his shot thumps off the backboard.

"Brick!" I yell. "Gimme my dollar!"

"Nah, nah, I meant to bet a candy bar," Sneaky says, grinning and shooting again even though it's my turn.

I make a few crazy shots, and before we know it, Sneaky's at *T*.

"*Hippopotamus*," he says.

"Nope," I tell him. "Beating you is gettin' boring."

Sneaky rolls his eyes and keeps shooting. I sit down on the bench and reach inside my backpack for Daddy's notebook. I feel words swirling in my head, but like always, they stay stuck inside. Instead, I read Daddy's story about Isaiah Dunn, Super-hero, playing in a championship basketball game.

"What you doing?" asks Sneaky. He holds the ball under his arm and gives me a weird look.

"Nothin'."

"Man, whatever," Sneaky says, throwing up another brick. "You and your little diary."

"You and your missed shots," I say, putting the notebook away before Sneaky can say anything else. "Ready to go home crying?"

"Yeah, right."

Sneaky shoots again and then sits down beside me.

"So when you guys gonna get a new place?" he asks.

I shrug. But when Sneaky opens a pack of Twizzlers and hands me one, I get an idea. It's not the greatest one, but it's the best I can come up with.

"We gotta get enough money for a new place," I tell Sneaky. "So I was thinking. What if I was your business partner?"

Sneaky pretends to choke on the Twizzler.

"I'm for real!" I say. I tell him about how I passed the caf-eteria during fourth-grade lunch and heard some kids yelling that the food sucked. I say that if someone could sneak in there, they'd probably make a ton of money. When I say "ton of money," Sneaky starts listening.

"I dunno, bro," he says, moving on to a lollipop.

"C'mon, Sneaky, it'll work," I tell him. "I really need to make some money so we can get a new place."

Sneaky sighs. "All right, man, guess I can give it a try. But we split everything sixty-forty."

"Cool," I say. It's better than nothing.

"Good." Sneaky grins and nudges me. "That means we gotta go to P.J.'s and stock up."

"Nah, man!" I groan. Sneaky knows I hate going over there. Last time, we bought candy at 7-Eleven, and Sneaky was mad because it cost us more.

"I ain't spending money like we did last time, 'Saiah," Sneaky tells me. I know he's right. But still.

"Man, Charlie's probably done by now," I tell him. Mama dropped us over here, like, an hour ago, and might be back already.

"Aight, let's go see," Sneaky says. I sigh and walk with him to the building.

"See, her car ain't here," Sneaky says. "Let's just go real quick, man."

"Okay, okay," I tell him. "But I'm not tryin' to take forever."

"I said real quick, right?" Sneaky grins, way too excited about this. I always hate buying candy, because I have to hand over money to do it.

We half walk, half run so it doesn't take us long to get to P.J.'s. I don't see Mama's car anywhere, which is good, but there's a bunch of guys standing around outside the store, and their eyes focus on me and Sneaky as we walk up. I swallow hard and grip the straps of my backpack as I follow Sneaky in.

We don't have to talk much, cuz we know the drill: Snickers, Milky Way, Now and Later, M&M's, Sour Patch Kids, Twizzlers. The same dude is working at the register and gives us a look when we dump the candy on the counter.

"Y'all got some kinda crazy sweet tooth or something?" he asks, ringing everything up.

"Nah," Sneaky says. I feel like we should say something else, but I don't know what, so I keep my mouth zipped.

"Fourteen seventy-three," the guy tells us, crossing his arms as me and Sneaky count the money. We split the cost of the candy, and I hate going into Daddy's sock to take out seven dollars and some change. We put the bags in my backpack before we leave the store. When we step outside, the same dudes are there.

"Ay, what y'all doing over here?" asks one of them. He looks like he's Antwan's age, and just as mean.

"Gettin' candy," Sneaky says.

"Y'all should do that over there," says another guy, pointing toward where Sneaky lives.

"Matter fact," says somebody else, "y'all go to Woodson, don't you?"

Aww, man. My stomach is really kicking now, cuz Creighton schools have always been rivals of Woodson schools.

"Man, we just came to get candy," Sneaky says, and we keep walking.

"Oh yeah? I think for being over here, y'all owe us some of that candy," the first guy says, and I feel a tug on my backpack. I jerk away hard. They all start laughing.

"Nah, man, they need to give us some of that money," says another guy. "There's a fee for y'all Woodson punks being over here."

I look over at Sneaky, and I hope he hears what I'm telling him, even though I don't say a thing. When the first guy reaches for my bag again, I spin around and take off.

Runnin' seems a whole lot easier when it's on a track somewhere, or when you're racing one of your friends. It's different when you're runnin', cuz somebody's chasing you. A *lot* of somebodies.

My book bag's thumping against my back with each step, everything inside slamming into my spine. Somehow Sneaky gets ahead of me. He turns a corner, then another, and I know that knife-stabbing feeling in my side is about to start up any second. But there's no way we can stop, not with all the footsteps and yelling behind us. I'm running so hard, after a while, I don't even notice sounds anymore.

"Over here!" Sneaky says finally, cutting into an alley. We crouch behind an old car and take deep breaths for a few minutes.

"Dang!" Sneaky says, coughing. I know why he says it, cuz it matches what I'm thinking: We ain't gettin' candy at P.J.'s anymore.

"We can find another spot," I tell him. Sneaky's definitely not good with that idea.

"Nah." He shakes his head. "Maybe we'll just come with Antwan next time."

"Why?" I ask. Sneaky stands up and doesn't look at me.

"They won't mess with us if we're with Antwan." Sneaky peeks around the car. "C'mon."

We walk back to the park, glancing over our shoulders, and I'm wondering about Antwan the whole time.

April 17

I DON'T CARE what Ms. Marlee says; I got nothing to say to Angel Atkins, and I'd be cool if she never says anything else to me. Ever.

But Mr. Tobin said we have to sit and talk and work out our issues in this stupid thing called Rocket ReStore with Ms. Marlee. Me and Mama had to listen to Mr. Tobin go on and on about the program; how peer counseling is so good, and how it's required once a kid gets suspended. And Mama actually signed the paper saying she agreed! I knew better than to complain, especially when she gave me a look and said I better not mess up again.

"Welcome, Isaiah," Ms. Marlee says when I come into her classroom, which looks more like a cozy bedroom, with chairs in every color you can think of. Angel's already there, and she turns away when she sees me. There's another kid in the room, and I guess he's supposed to be our peer counselor. I'd be mad if I were him, having to be at school all early when you're not even in trouble.

"You can have a seat wherever you'd like," Ms. Marlee says. I pick an orange chair, far from Angel. I notice a pink notebook at her feet, but she kicks it under her chair when she sees me looking at it.

"So are you related to Bob Marley?" Angel asks, all rude.

"Not that I know of," Ms. Marlee says. "Our last names are actually spelled differently. But who knows, we might be! I do love singing!"

Angel doesn't say anything to that. She seems disappointed

that Ms. Marlee didn't get rude back. Ms. Marlee's like sunshine to Angel's ugly rain clouds.

"So . . ." Ms. Marlee claps her hands. "Isaiah, Angel, you probably don't know Tayshaun, so I'll let him introduce himself and why he's here."

"Hey, everyone, I'm Tayshaun Peterson," he says. "I'm in seventh grade. Last year, I got into a lot of fights and didn't really do my work. I had to do the whole Rocket ReStore thing, and I thought it was gonna suck at first. But once we all started talking about stuff, things got better. Now I'm friends with some of the guys I used to fight with."

I think about what Tayshaun's saying, but I can't ever imagine being friends with Angel. Her face looks like she's thinking the same thing.

When Tayshaun's done, Ms. Marlee talks about Rocket ReStore, and she's saying all the same stuff Mr. Tobin did. But when she says the *R* in *ReStore* stands for *Respect,* she looks right at Angel.

"Everyone in this room has value, and we will speak to each other in a way that shows we believe that."

I look at Angel and try to imagine what value she has. I can't think of anything.

"So, Isaiah, what do you know about Angel?" asks Tayshaun.

I stare at my feet.

"Ummm, I don't know."

"Take a few seconds to think about it," Ms. Marlee says. "One thing you know about her."

I think about how Angel's sneakers are pink, and she usually has a pink headband or ponytail holder. And the notebook.

"Ummm, she likes pink?"

"Good," says Ms. Marlee. "That's a great observation. Now, Angel. What's one thing you know about Isaiah?"

I look down again and try to stay cool, cuz even though Ms. Marlee said we have to respect each other, I just know Angel ain't gonna listen.

"He likes writing," Angel says, "but he don't do it anymore."

"How you know that?" The words fly out of my mouth before I even think about it. Angel doesn't say anything, but Ms. Marlee does.

"You'd be surprised how much you two really know about each other, and how much you have in common."

I think about Angel shopping in Seven Baskets and wonder if her family's in a motel, too. I wonder if she has a dad.

Ms. Marlee asks us questions about what's going on with the two of us, and why we don't get along so good. At first, neither of us talks too much; I guess no one wants to snitch.

"Why do you feel you can't get along with Angel?" Ms. Marlee asks me.

"She always talking 'bout me," I finally say. "For no reason."

"No, I'm not!" Angel shoots back.

"Angel, let's respect Isaiah's feelings," Ms. Marlee says. "Have you said mean things about him, or called him names?"

"No," Angel says, but she hangs her head, and we all know she's lying.

"We'll give you a few minutes to think about it, Angel," Ms. Marlee says. "No one likes being teased."

"Oh yeah?" Angel looks up and narrows her eyes. "Well, Isaiah ran his mouth about me, too!"

"What?! I never said anything about you!" I say. I wanna tell Ms. Marlee and Tayshaun, "See? Angel's mean *and* she lies!"

"Isaiah, let's respect Angel and let her finish," Ms. Marlee says.

I cross my arms and narrow my eyes right back at Angel.

"Last year in Ms. Harrison's class," Angel says, "you said that poem about my hair to Sneaky."

Huh?

"Isaiah, do you know what Angel is referring to?"

"No," I say.

"'Look at that on Angel's head; looks just like a rat that's dead!'"

When Angel says it, I remember. It was at recess, after Ms. Harrison had read us poems in class. I said it to Sneaky, and we laughed. I didn't know Angel had heard me.

"Did you say that?" Tayshaun asks.

"Yeah," I say, feeling pretty bad, especially when I take a peek at Angel's face. "But I didn't mean for her to hear me."

"Well, she did, Isaiah," Ms. Marlee says. "And it seems like it really hurt her feelings."

I want to tell Angel sorry, but I remember all the mean things she's said to me, and how it's hurt *my* feelings, so I don't say anything.

Ms. Marlee tells us we're done for today. Two meetings to go. Before I leave, I see Angel reach under her chair and grab the pink notebook. She holds it super close, the same way I do with Daddy's.

April 18

MR. SHEPHARD'S GRINNING up a storm when I walk into the children's section of the library.

"Isaiah Dunn, Superstar!" he says, holding his fist out.

"What's up, Mr. S," I say, heading for my table by the window. I drop my bag on the table and dig around inside for Daddy's notebook. Only forty pages left now. I've been trying not to read so fast, but it's, like, the only thing to do at Smoky Inn. Before I sit down, I notice that Mr. Shephard's still standing there, giving me a funny look.

"Well?" he asks.

"Well what?" I say, scrunching up my face.

"You're really gonna keep me in suspense?" Mr. Shephard shakes his head. "What did your dad say?"

"Huh?" Now I really give Mr. S a look.

"You don't know? After bugging me for weeks and weeks?"

That's when I realize what he's talking about. The contest. By the way Mr. Shephard's grinning, it's gotta be good news! My heart starts racing with excitement.

"What happened? Did we win?"

"They announced it yesterday," Mr. Shephard says. He raises an eyebrow. "You guys don't check email?"

"I forgot," I tell Mr. Shephard. I don't say that the past few days have been not-good days for Mama. "Who won?"

Mr. Shephard shakes his head, the smile still on his face. It's *gotta* be good, but he's not saying. He points to the computers.

"You gotta see for yourself," he says.

I move like the Flash to the computers and log in to my email, IMDunn@woodsonrockets.org. Even though it's my school account, I'm still surprised to see Daddy's name.

Dear Gary Dunn,
    Congratulations! Your short story was selected as the second-place winner in our 17th annual Short Stack Contest!

My eyes dance across the page as I read the rest of the email from Friends of the Hamilton Plaza Library. Daddy won second place! I look over at Mr. S, and this time, my grin is as big as his.

"Can I print this?" I ask. I can't wait to show Mama! I know that even if she had another not-good day, this will make it all better.

"Of course!" Mr. S says. "Your pops is library famous!"

Once the email's printed, I read the whole thing again.

"What's a reception?" I ask Mr. Shephard, reading that there's gonna be one on May 2.

"Oh, that's just a special dinner where they officially give your dad the award." Mr. Shephard pats me on the back. "You guys'll have to break out the fancy tuxedos!"

I swallow hard. Mr. Shephard doesn't know about Daddy; nobody at the library does. I'm thinking maybe if they found out, they'd take back the award.

"But, um, what if my dad can't, um, make it?" I ask Mr. Shephard.

"To the reception?" Mr. Shephard raises an eyebrow. "I'm sure he'll want to be there. Your whole family can come."

When I don't say anything, Mr. Shephard asks, "Everything okay? Does your dad know you entered his story?"

"No," I say. I stare at the piece of paper in my hand. "My dad, he, um, he passed away. On Thanksgiving."

That's the first time I've ever said it out loud. I've never even said it to Sneaky.

"I'm so sorry to hear that," Mr. Shephard says with a sigh, and when I finally look up at him, I can tell he means it. Not like some other people who just say the words because they're supposed to.

Mr. Shephard sits down beside me, and I tell him how one minute we were walking around downtown, huddled close and enjoying the Thanksgiving Day parade in the freezing cold. The next minute, Daddy was falling, and Mama was screaming, and Charlie was crying, and I couldn't move. People standing close to us were watching, their faces shocked. But other people, further ahead, had no clue what had happened, and their faces were still smiling and happy. I remember looking up and seeing one lady with a purple scarf, laughing so hard she had to hold on to the guy standing next to her. She couldn't see us; couldn't see Daddy on the ground. And I stayed mad at purple-scarf lady for a long time.

"The ambulance came, and so did Miz Rita," I tell Mr. Shephard. "We stayed at her place that night, but I didn't go to sleep."

Mr. Shephard nods, just letting me talk.

"Mama came the next afternoon, and I knew."

I tell Mr. Shephard it was a heart attack, which is a weird

thing to call it, cuz what is it that attacks your heart anyway? Daddy not being here is what attacks my heart; Mama and Charlie's too. All three of us are having heart attacks.

I tell Mr. Shephard about how I found Daddy's notebook and typed up one of his stories for the contest, but I don't say anything about us staying at the Smoky Inn and how the money can help us get our place back. Mr. Shephard listens until I'm done, and then he sits down right beside me.

"Isaiah, what you did was amazing," he tells me. "You are very strong, and I know your dad would be very proud of you."

I wait for the "but," the part when he tells me that Daddy's story can't be the winner anymore. But Mr. Shephard doesn't say that at all.

"I lost my pops when I was thirteen," he says. "And you know what I did?"

"What?"

"I stopped talking."

I give Mr. Shephard a "Huh?" look, and he nods.

"Yeah, man, I just stopped talking altogether. Quiet as a church mouse."

"Why'd you do that?" I ask.

"I don't know," Mr. Shephard says. "Nothing I could say— nothing anybody could say—would bring him back. So I thought, why say anything?"

I nod slowly, thinking about how my words stopped coming to me after Daddy died.

"How long did you not talk?"

"A month, maybe," Mr. Shephard says. "Wanna know what my first words were?"

"What?" I ask. Mr. Shephard smiles.

" 'This real good.' "

"That's what you said?"

"That's what I said. The lady who used to watch my siblings and me after school made this peach cobbler one day, and after I took that first bite, I couldn't stay quiet anymore!"

Mr. Shephard stands up to get back to work.

"I gotta say, you're doing much better at honoring your pops than I did, Isaiah. Congrats again."

"Thanks," I say, reading the email one more time.

When Mama picks me up, it's the first thing I show her. Her eyes get huge and she gasps, all surprised.

"He won, Isaiah? Daddy won?" she asks, sounding as excited as me.

"Well, it's second place, but yeah, he won!" I say. "I told you he was good!"

"I can't believe it!"

"What happened?" asks Charlie, mad cuz she can't read all the words in the email.

"Your brother entered one of Daddy's stories in a contest, and it won second place!"

"What does he win?" Charlie asks. Then she scrunches up her face. "Wait, how can he get anything?"

"Well, no, sweetie, Daddy can't get anything now," Mama says, reaching back to squeeze Charlie's hand. "But *we* can get it for him."

And we start planning for the reception right there in the library parking lot. Mama sounds like herself again, like Daddy's win told her it's all gonna be okay.

April 19

"SO WHAT'S IN the notebook?" I ask Angel. Mrs. Fisher just told us to get into our poetry groups and work on our projects, and since Angel doesn't roll her eyes when I scoot my chair next to her, I figure it's cool if I ask her. Plus, Ms. Marlee said we should always ask questions instead of assuming.

"Stuff," Angel says.

"Like what?"

"Whatever I feel like writing. What do you write in yours?"

"Nothing," I say. "I don't write anymore."

"Why not?" Angel asks. I shrug. She might be getting nicer

because of Rocket ReStore, but I bet she'll be back to her normal self after our last session, which is later today.

"Well, I hate quitting stuff," Angel tells me. Ouch. When I don't say anything, she starts talking about our project. We're gonna pick some famous poems, cut out all the words, and rearrange them into new poems. We call it Poetry Transformers.

We get on our Chromebooks and start typing the poems, and Angel's way faster than me. She gets through two poems while I'm still typing my first one.

"You slow," she says, but the grin on her face is definitely not her usual mean mug.

"Well, how 'bout you type and print them, and I'll cut out the words?" I suggest. Angel's cool with my idea, and we get into a good groove with the project. She even writes some of the poems herself, cuz she's got this neat, bubbly handwriting.

"This one's funny," Angel says when she types up the poem "Snowball" by Shel Silverstein. "Who would put a snowball in their bed?"

I cut out each word of the poem, already imagining how I would rearrange them for a new poem. When I get to "Harlem" by Langston Hughes, I think about my notebook, how my words are drying up like raisins, only it's in my head, not the sun. I think about what Angel said about quitting. I know Daddy wouldn't want any of that to happen.

"Poems."

"Huh?"

"I used to write poems," I tell Angel. Something tells me it's okay to say it. Daddy used to tell me that once you speak positive, positive things will happen. But what if he's wrong; what if Angel laughs and teases me even more? I don't know if I could be sunshine to her rain clouds if that happens.

"I like poems," Angel says. She turns and gives me a look with narrowed eyes. "*Except* the one you made about my hair."

"Sorry," I say, and mean it.

"Umm-hmm," Angel says, using markers to write words on a sheet of paper. Her lips are kinda poked out like she's got an attitude, but at least she doesn't say anything mean. She doesn't say she's sorry, either, and I almost wanna take mine back.

"Very good work, Angel and Isaiah," Mrs. Fisher says, walking by our table. She smiles, and when she moves on, Angel rolls her eyes.

"Can't stand her," she says under her breath. I smile a little. Guess that's something else we have in common.

Later, when I'm reading one of Daddy's stories in 109, I feel words coming.

"Don't let 'em dry up like a raisin in the sun," I whisper. Charlie's in my bed, and she's supposed to be sleeping.

I'm staying up until Mama comes back from the Smoky Inn office.

"Are you talking to yourself, 'Saiah?" Charlie asks, looking at me like I'm crazy.

"No," I tell her. "Words are talking to *me*."

"Nuh-uhhh!" Charlie says. "Words don't talk!"

"Yeah, they do."

I reach in my backpack for a pen, and I write my words next to Daddy's:

IN COMMON

we are different, but the same,
sometimes sunshine, sometimes rain.
If we see
who we are,
we won't be
very far.

April 22

MY PRAYERS MUST be working, cuz Mama drops me off on time at Laser Zone for Sneaky's birthday party. She even took me to the store so I could use some of my candy money to get a present for him: a basketball hoop to put on the back of his bedroom door. Hint, hint, practice needed!

"Isaiah, I wanna come!" whines Charlie when I open the car door. I feel a little bad for leaving her, but no way do I want to chase her around Laser Zone all day.

"I'll get you something," I tell her.

"Promise?" Charlie asks.

"Of course," I say, popping my collar, hero-style. Charlie laughs, and I run inside.

"Yo, what's up, 'Saiah?" Sneaky's the first to see me, and he's already hyped for laser tag. We do our special handshake, and Sneaky adds some extra moves at the end, probably to impress Aliya.

"What's that, the candy boy shake?" asks Aliya, with a smirk.

"Hey, no selling candy at your party," says Gabi. "We already bought you presents!"

"I'm hurt," Sneaky says, pretending to be sad. "There will be no business operations at this party, Gabriella."

"Good!" Aliya says, like it's her party.

"But yo, Isaiah, we should make our own dance! Call it the candy boy shake!" Sneaky grins.

"Yeah, thanks for the idea, Aliya!" I say. Aliya groans, but I can tell she wants to watch what we come up with.

There's already loud music playing, so me and Sneaky start the dance with our handshake.

"Then how 'bout this?" Sneaky says, making a motion like he's counting dollars. I add a move that's like popping M&M's into my mouth, and then we do one where we throw candy to the audience. No lie, everybody stops what they're doing to watch us, especially when we try it the second time and it's much smoother. Greg, Kiki, and Jules are the first to try the candy boy shake, then Gabi and Mike O. Aliya stands with her arms crossed, telling us how bad we look, until she realizes she's the only one not dancing. Then she's got no choice but to join us. Even Sneaky's mom tries out our moves, which is pretty funny.

"I didn't know you could dance," Gabi tells me after we're all done.

"I got some moves," I say, shrugging.

"Yo, y'all should let me record you and upload it to You-Tube!" says Jules, pulling out his iPhone.

"We tired, man; hold on," says Sneaky, flopping on the floor all dramatic.

"I'm just sayin'," Jules tells him, "y'all could blow up!"

"Ugh, don't tell them that, Jules," says Aliya, rolling her eyes. "That wack dance wasn't all that."

"Hater!" laughs Sneaky. I laugh, too, cuz Aliya really is hatin', and she knows it.

"Well, if this was gonna be a dance party, I could've done that in my living room!" says Sneaky's mom. "What did I pay this place for?"

"It's all good, Ma, we're gonna play," Sneaky assures her, pulling me to arcade games.

Sneaky's definitely better at air hockey than he is at basketball. We play three games, and he gets me every time.

"You need some lessons!" laughs Aliya when she takes my place at the table. She's good like Sneaky, and they both win a game before Sneaky takes the tiebreaker.

"Okay, you and me," I tell Sneaky, heading toward the basketball game.

"Nah, I'm tired," Sneaky says, faking a yawn.

"Tired of getting beat!" I laugh. I beat Sneaky, then Jules, then Aliya. It's a close game with Gabi, but I beat her, too. I stuff the tickets in my pocket, already thinking about what I'll get for Charlie.

"Pizza time!" calls Sneaky's mom, and we all take off for the tables.

"Bet I can eat the most pizza," says Jules.

"Yeah, whatever," says Sneaky, his mouth already stuffed.

"How 'bout this," says Mike O, "whoever wins gets everyone else's tickets."

"I'm not in it," says Gabi.

"Yeah, you not getting my tickets," Kiki says.

"What about you?" Jules asks me. I feel the pile of tickets in my pocket and think about a prize for Charlie. But then I think I could get her something *really* good if I win more tickets.

"I'm in," I say, picking up my second slice.

"You guys are gross," says Kiki as we pile the pizza into our mouths. "Please don't puke all over the table!"

Sneaky pretends to cough, and Kiki moves to another seat.

"How many slices you on?" Mike O asks.

"Four," says Sneaky.

"Five," Aliya says, sticking out her tongue at Sneaky.

"What about you, 'Saiah?" Sneaky asks. He looks like he's slowing down, so I'm glad to share my number.

"Seven."

"What?! No way!"

"For real," I say, laughing. What they don't know is that I didn't eat breakfast, and I haven't had pizza in months!

"Aww, man, I'm done," groans Aliya. Her eyes bug open when I grab my eighth slice.

"Aight, aight, Isaiah wins," Sneaky says. "I never wanna eat pizza again!"

Everyone hands over their tickets, and I feel like I just won in Vegas. Yes!

We sing "Happy Birthday" to Sneaky and watch him open his presents. Before we leave, I head to the prize counter and try to imagine what Charlie would want.

"What about that dog?" Sneaky says.

"Nah, that ain't Charlie," I say. I keep looking, and then I see the perfect prize. I hand over all my tickets for a pink notebook and pen set. The notebook kinda looks like Angel's, and I wonder if she got hers from here, too. I hope Charlie likes it as much as Angel likes hers. At least now Charlie can stop scribbling in all my stuff.

"What is it with you guys and notebooks?" Sneaky asks.

"Don't hate," I tell him.

We do our handshake before I walk outside, heart thumping a little cuz I wonder if Mama will be on time. I breathe a sigh of relief when she pulls up a few seconds later.

"'Saiah, what you get me?" Charlie asks, bouncing in her seat.

"Aww, man!" I slap my hand to my forehead. "I forgot all about that, Charlie!"

Charlie pouts and crosses her arms in front of her chest, all attitude. Can't help but laugh.

"I'm just messin' with you," I say, handing her the notebook and pen.

"Whoa!" Charlie squeals. "This is spectacular!"

Me and Mama laugh, cuz Charlie's started this thing where she hears a big word and then repeats it as much as she can.

"Thanks, Isaiah Dunn, Superhero," she says.

I gotta admit, I do feel like a hero the whole drive back.

April 24

THIRTY-EIGHT DOLLARS AND fourteen cents.

That's all I got crumpled up in Daddy's sock. I pour the coins and dollar bills back onto the bathroom floor of 109 and count it again. Nothing changes. Thirty-eight dollars and fourteen cents is nice, but it's not enough. I gotta get more money. Only problem is, I have no ideas. Sneaky's mom gives him an allowance, plus money on his birthday and at Christmas. Combine that with his candy hustle, and he's set. I know for sure Mama won't be giving me any kind of allowance, and my birthday's two months away.

Selling candy to the fourth graders has been okay; but Mrs. Fisher doesn't always give me a pass for the bathroom, so I have to sit in class, watching the minutes and the chances for dollars tick by. Sneaky says we have to come up with a good reason for me to leave the class every day, like a doctor's note or something. I know I can't depend on just the candy money, though. I need an idea that's all mine.

I sit with my back to the door and Daddy's notebook in my hand, and it makes me feel close to him, like if I need anything, I'll get it in the notebook.

"So what would you do if you needed money?" I ask quietly, flipping through the pages. I start thinking about Daddy's job, and how he worked a lot at night, making sure buildings were clean. I stop flipping pages when I see some words that have nothing to do with "The Beans and Rice Chronicles of Isaiah Dunn." The words kinda look like the words *I* write. Poems. I run my fingers over the words *Black Sand* and read:

Who tucks these tiny jewels of light
In a perfect blanket of Black Sand
Every night
The same way
I tuck my precious jewels in tight?

I wonder if Daddy got tired of stories for a second and just let his words come out differently, the way I do. I read his poem over and over, and think about how he used to tuck me and Charlie in and say, "Good night, my precious jewel." I would groan and beg him not to call me a jewel, cuz that's for girls, so then he started saying, "My strong prince."

Thinking about all of this makes me remember asking him once how he could stay awake all night, and he told me he was used to it. "When I was your age," he'd said, "I was already working two jobs. And here you are, complaining about waking up for school!"

That's it!

I squeeze my eyes shut and try to remember what Daddy's

two jobs were when he was my age. I picture us at the kitchen table, me drinking hot chocolate, about to go to sleep, and him drinking coffee, about to go to work. I see his smile, the way he moved his hands when he talked, the sound of his voice.

And then I remember.

Daddy delivered papers in the morning, and helped in a barbershop after school.

Yes! I grin at the notebook as if it was Daddy's face. Now I have a plan, at least.

"'Saiah, open up, I gotta use it!" Charlie's annoying whine yanks me from my thoughts. She bangs on the door, and I feel the pounding in my back. She's gonna wake Mama up with all that noise.

"Hold on!" I tell her, stuffing the notebook and money sock into my backpack and zipping it up. When I open the door, she's standing there doing the potty dance, sucking on her fingers. She darts in around me and doesn't even close the door.

"Gross, Charlie!" I say, hearing her grunt. I shut the door, but she starts complaining.

"No! Leave it open! It's scary in here, 'Saiah."

Charlie was never scared in our other bathroom.

"Don't worry," I tell her, peeking in. "We won't be here much longer, Charlie. No more scary places."

I leave the door cracked and fix the sofa bed, storing my

backpack underneath. I think about Daddy's words in the note-book, the words about the jewels in the blanket of black sand. And I wish he was here to tuck me in, even if he wanted to call me a jewel.

April 25

I'M PRETTY SURE they don't do the paperboy thing anymore, so instead of walking to the library after school, I go three blocks over to New Growth, the place where Sneaky gets his hair cut. I figure I can still try Daddy's other job.

A dude with bulging muscles gives me a nod when I come in. He's busy shaping up somebody's baby fro, and there are a few people waiting in chairs.

"Here for a cut, li'l man?"

"Um, no," I say. "I'm looking for Rock." At lunch today, Sneaky told me the only barber he knows is Rock. He said Rock is all about the business, and out of everyone in the shop, he cuts hair the best.

The guy looks up at me, then back to his customer's head, a smirk on his face.

"You lookin' for Rock? And why would you be doing that?"

"Uh." I swallow hard, noticing the skull tattoo on the guy's arm. "Cuz I need to make some money."

The guy—I'm pretty sure he's Rock—switches off his clippers, narrows his eyes, and stares at me. A lady who's braiding hair looks up like, "Uh-oh, look out!" and shakes her head.

"You need to make some money? What, you got bills to pay and mouths to feed?"

"He probably tryin' to buy that expensive phone," says an old guy waiting for a cut. "That thang 'bout as much as my mortgage!"

People in the shop chuckle, and the guy goes back to his haircut. I don't move from where I'm standing. I'm thinking about Daddy and wondering if it was this hard for him to get his barbershop job.

"That what it is, li'l man?" asks the guy, leaning in as he lines his customer up. "Cell phone or sneakers?"

I shake my head, decide to be honest.

"Gotta help my mama," I say. I watch the black tufts of hair falling to the floor. "I could come after school and sweep up hair and stuff."

The guy doesn't say anything right away. He cuts his clippers off again, brushes off his customer's neck, and hands him a mirror. "Check that out, D."

The guy named D studies himself and grins, gently patting his fro. He gives his barber some green.

"It's nice and crispy like always, Rock," he says, all smiles. I smile, too, cuz now I know that Rock is Rock.

"That's how I do, brotha," Rock says. D leaves the barber-shop, checking his reflection in every mirror he walks by. Rock brushes his clippers off and sprays them before saying anything else to me.

"Come over here, li'l man, I don't bite," Rock says, arranging his equipment nice and neat. I take a few steps closer and notice that Rock has some gray hairs in his beard, just like Daddy did.

"So, you helping your moms, huh?" he asks. Once he's done with his clippers, he sits in the chair and studies me.

I nod, not really sure what I should say.

"That's what's up. I respect that," Rock says, holding out his fist to give me dap. "But listen, li'l man, around here, we sweep up ourselves, you know?"

"Oh," I say, and suddenly the hole in my sneakers is real interesting to look at.

"I'll tell you what, though," says Rock, leaning in close to me. "Don't tell her I said this, but my wife? She's the real boss around here. She ran down the street to get some wings, but when she comes back, you can pitch your idea to her. If you can win her over, man, we'll see what we can do. Fair enough?"

I nod again, hoping his wife isn't like Mrs. Fisher at school.

"You gonna have to do more than nodding with her, though, aight?" Rock stands up, grabs a broom, and starts sweeping up the hair. I take a deep breath and mentally tell my stomach to relax. I don't have time to figure out what I'm gonna say, cuz just a second later, the door opens and in walks a lady holding a bag from Wings2Go. Gotta be Rock's wife. Rock opens his mouth to say something, but Isaiah Dunn, Superhero beats him to it.

"Mrs. Rock, do you see what your husband's doing?" I say, a little louder than I should have. Feels like the whole shop is staring at me now.

"What?" Mrs. Rock raises an eyebrow, and even Rock looks a little confused, like, "Dude, what are you *doin'*?"

"Your husband," I say, pointing to Rock. "You see what he's doing?"

"Uh, yeah." Mrs. Rock gives Rock a who-is-this-kid? look. "He's cleaning up all this hair."

"Yeah, but do you know what he *should* be doing?" I ask.

"Rock, who is this?" Mrs. Rock asks.

"I'm tryin' to figure that out myself, baby," Rock answers. I swallow hard.

"He *should* be about to eat those wings with you," I tell her. "And if you had somebody to sweep up this hair, that's what he'd be doing right now!"

The room goes library quiet, and then all of a sudden, Rock cracks up laughing.

"I see you, kid!" he says, holding his fist toward me again. "You ain't playin', are you?"

"He came with it!" calls out the old guy who said I just wanted a phone.

Mrs. Rock still looks clueless, so Rock tells her I'm looking for a job to help Mama out at home.

"What's your name, li'l man?" Rock asks. I open my mouth to answer, but somebody beats me to it.

"Isaiah?"

Me, Rock, and Mrs. Rock all turn around and see a lady in the back poking her head out from underneath a hair dryer. It's Miz Rita! I didn't even notice her over there.

"Hi, Miz Rita," I say.

"I didn't know that was you, baby," she says, waving me over. "How you been?"

"Good," I tell her.

"Miz Rita, you know this young man?" asks Mrs. Rock.

"Do I know him?" Miz Rita makes a *pssst* sound. "Only since he was in Pull-Ups."

I groan and put a hand over my face. "C'mon, Miz Rita!"

"So I shouldn't be worried that he's trying to get a job in my shop?" asks Rock.

Miz Rita's eyes bounce to mine.

"A job?"

I nod. She doesn't say anything, but she studies me real hard.

"Well, he'd be a good worker for you, that's for sure," Miz Rita says. "His friend, Sneaky, though, that's another story!"

"You friends with Sneaky?" asks Rock.

"Yeah," I say.

"That kid is something else! Came here selling candy one day before I cut his hair." Rock laughs and shakes his head. "I will say this, though, it's good to see y'all young guys hustlin' the right way."

Rock hands me the broom and grabs his wife's arm. "We gonna make sure these wings are talkin' 'bout something, and then you and me can talk business."

I start sweeping up the hair, and I can't help but grin.

April 28

MY STOMACH FEELS like Jackie Chan is inside, kicking up a storm. Me and Angel have to present our poetry project, and even though it only has to be three minutes long, that seems like forever to me! We met up at the library a few times to practice, and Mr. Shephard kept telling us we're gonna do fine. I think he's just saying that cuz he has to.

"You aight?" Angel asks me. I can't lie; the whole Rocket ReStore thing did help me and Angel. We're not best friends or anything, but we don't feel like enemies, either.

"Yeah," I say, but the truth is, I'm feelin' real nervous, like something's not gonna go how we practiced. Mrs. Fisher calls our names, and we walk to the front and set up our giant poster, which is filled with the words from all the poems we liked. The words are big and little, some typed and some written in Angel's bubble letters, and in all colors.

"When we're little, one of the first things we learn is the alphabet. Those twenty-six letters make up the millions of words we use, and those words can form anything we want, including poems." Angel starts off our presentation, and it doesn't seem like she's nervous at all. She reads some of the poems we picked, and the sound of the words helps me calm down.

I picture the words we pulled from "Snowball" by Shel Silverstein: *Snowball. Pillow. Sleep.* And from "Harlem" by Langston Hughes: *Dream. Sugar. Sun. Explode.* The class laughs when Angel reads "Poor Old Lady and Homework! Oh Homework!" I spot the words on our poster board: *Fly. Bird. Lady. Die. Horse. Wash. Dark. See. Bomb.*

Once Angel's done, I have to read the new poems we created from all the words. I look down to make sure my note cards are in order, and then I freeze. I'm supposed to have five cards, but there are only three in my hand. I shuffle through them again, but the number doesn't change.

"And now, Isaiah will show you how words can do whatever you need them to."

Angel's voice sounds far away, and I am glued to my spot like Anna in the movie *Frozen,* which I've seen a thousand times with Charlie.

"Ummm, Isaiah?" Angel gives me a look.

"Huh?" I snap out of it. "Oh, um, hold on a second."

I dash from the front of the class to our table and unzip my backpack. As I'm digging around inside, I remember Charlie playing with my cards last night. But when I snatched them from her, I thought I had them all. My heart sinks; Angel's gonna be so mad at me. Maybe she'll go back to being mean. My fingers brush Daddy's notebook, and that makes me imagine myself as Isaiah Dunn, Superhero. I don't have a bowl of beans and rice, but I do have my daddy's words. I take a few quick breaths and walk back to the front, carrying the notebook with me.

"What we did is kinda like magic," I say. I look over, and Angel's face is like, "What are you doing?"

"Think about it: All these words made up the poems Angel read." I point at the poster. "But they also can be used for new poems. Like this."

I study the board, taking in all the words. I know I have to think super fast. Lucky for me, the words fly toward me like a fastball in baseball.

"Dreams are snow, new every year, and useful even when they stop falling."

I make up another poem about an exploding sandwich, and everyone laughs. I ask if anyone else wants to try, and Mike O gives it a shot.

"Um, I walk with the snowman, whose eyes are raisins, and

the sun melts him into a bed of, ummm"—Mike O stares at the board for a word—"a bed of moonlight!"

Mike O takes a bow while everyone claps. Even Mrs. Fisher tries a poem. After that, Angel ends our presentation. When I sit down, I feel like I just hit a game-winning shot in basketball.

Right before recess Mrs. Fisher tells me and Angel that we did an excellent job.

"It was so creative!" she says with a huge smile on her face. "And I'm so proud of the way you worked together!"

Angel pokes her lips out, but she doesn't say anything smart.

"You know, we should really have a poetry club here at Woodson," Mrs. Fisher continues. "Would you two be interested in starting one?"

"We'll think about it," Angel says.

"Please do!" Mrs. Fisher says, moving on to talk to someone else.

I don't tell Angel this, but along with the A we just got, I also like the way she says "we'll."

May 2

THE RECEPTION ROOM at the library is small—which is good—but packed with people, which is *not* good. Mr. Shephard meets us at the door and shows us which table's ours. He promises I won't have to talk, but I'm still nervous. Charlie squeals when she sees her full name in fancy letters on a card by her plate.

Charlise Dunn

"Look, Mama! It's my whole name!" she says.

"This is so nice!" Mama says, scanning the room and smiling. She's wearing a pretty dress the color of grape juice, and before we got here, she kept complaining that the dress was showing all her "rolls," even though I told her she looked awesome.

"Well, we love to honor our writers." Mr. Shephard winks and fist-bumps me. "You guys sit down and relax. You'll be able to get your food in just a minute."

I turn around and see steaming-hot serving trays lined up on a table against the wall. In my mind, I pray real hard that there's no beans and rice over there!

"How come I have two forks?" Charlie asks loudly.

"Shhh!" I tell her. Mama doesn't seem to mind. She tells Charlie one fork's for the salad and one's for the dinner.

"Well, aren't you handsome, young man!" says a lady who's sitting at our table. "That's quite a tie you have on."

"Thanks," I say, touching the tie. It's too big for me, but I don't care. It's Daddy's, and I told Mama I had to have him with me today.

"What about my dress?" Charlie asks, jumping up from her seat and twirling. The lady laughs.

"Your dress is lovely!" she says. "All three of you look so beautiful."

"Charlie, sit down!" I hiss, cuz the girl won't stop spinning around! Luckily, someone comes to tell us our table can go get food. Mama and the lady talk while we go through the line, and I help Charlie put food on her plate.

"This smells so good!" Charlie's as excited as me to see the salad, corn, baked chicken, mashed potatoes with tons of gravy, and soft, buttery rolls. We don't even mind the green beans!

The program starts while we're eating. A bunch of important people talk about the library and all its programs, but I don't pay much attention. I'm too busy making sure Charlie doesn't knock over the candle that's in the middle of the table. I wonder if I have time to get seconds before I have to go up for Daddy's award.

"And now, ladies and gentlemen, to introduce our short-story contest winners, here's Marsha Priest, president of the Hamilton Plaza Library Literacy Foundation!"

The audience claps politely, and my mouth drops open when the lady from our table stands up and walks to the front. I gulp, hoping she didn't think Charlie was too annoying.

Mrs. Priest starts by thanking everyone for coming to celebrate good writing. I feel warm inside. She's talking about Daddy!

"I promise, I read each and every story, and loved them all. But the three winners we honor tonight are nothing short of brilliant. Please join me in celebrating our third-place winner, Gordon Jeffries!"

We all clap as Mr. Jeffries, a pretty old dude, grins as he walks to the front of the room. Mama reaches over Charlie and squeezes my hand. I squeeze back and pretend to be Isaiah Dunn, Superhero, who's not scared of anything.

"Ladies and gentlemen, let's give a round of applause to our second-place winner, Gary Dunn, whom we honor posthumously tonight. His wonderful son, Isaiah, submitted his piece and will be accepting the award on his behalf."

Everyone starts clapping as I stand up. I see Mr. Shephard clapping and whistling, and I hear Charlie shout, "Yay, Isaiah!"

I make it to the front without tripping, and smile big when they take a picture of me and Mrs. Priest with the award. After the picture, Mrs. Priest hands me an envelope and whispers in my ear, "Make sure you give this to your mom."

I walk back to our table with the envelope and the award, which is in the shape of an open notebook. I hand both to Mama. I know the prize money isn't as much as first place, but it will still help.

Mama runs her fingers over Daddy's name on the award and

smiles. We all clap big for the first-place winner, and then the library staff passes out cake and ice cream. I try to hold on to the sweetness for a long time, cuz it'll probably be a while before I get ice cream again.

"Isaiah, we are just so proud of you!" Mrs. Priest comes back to the table right after I stuffed my face with a huge bite of cake. She turns to Mama next, so I don't have to talk right away.

"Mrs. Dunn, I am very sorry for your loss," she says, and I stop chewing. Why would she say that? Doesn't she know it will only make Mama get sad? I watch Mama's face closely as she gives Mrs. Priest a small smile.

"Thank you so much," she tells Mrs. Priest. "Things have definitely been tough. But Isaiah's doing a great job of keeping his dad with us."

That makes me feel good. And as other people come up and tell us the same thing Mrs. Priest did, Mama's smile gets bigger and bigger. Mine, too.

Thanks, Daddy.

May 6

"YO, WE GOTTA do our routine to this," Sneaky says, playing a Bruno Mars song on his cell phone.

"That one's cool," I say. We decided to enter our school's

talent show and do the candy boy shake. Sneaky thinks it'll make us famous, and he wants to practice, like, ALL the time.

Mama musta known I needed a break from Charlie, cuz she dropped me off to hang with Sneaky while she and Charlie visit a free gymnastics class. I think Mama taking Charlie to stuff like that is a good sign that things are getting better.

After an hour of practice, Sneaky's ready for a break. His mom is busy watching a movie in the living room, and Antwan is out with his friends, so we have the room to ourselves. Before he turns on his PlayStation, Sneaky goes to his closet, digs around, and comes back with a bag of Doritos.

"Aight, let's go," he says, putting in *NBA 2K19*. He picks the Lakers, and he beats my Pistons.

"Yo, that's the only way you ever win at basketball," I say. I see the basketball hoop I got him up on his door, and I feel good that he's using it.

"Don't hate, dude," Sneaky says, crunching on a handful of chips and restarting the game. We play again, and this time my Pistons beat Sneaky's Knicks.

"Why you always pick the Pistons, bro?" Sneaky asks when I pick them again for our third game.

"They're my team," I tell him.

"Your dad liked them, too, right?" Sneaky asks. "That's probably why you like them."

"I guess."

I think about this dude Daddy always talked about, Isiah Thomas. He said Isiah Thomas was an awesome basketball player, one of the best. Daddy liked him so much, he named me after him! Mama said they went back and forth about my name, even in the delivery room before I was born. Finally, Mama gave in, but she told Daddy they had to spell my name the Bible way.

Daddy used to have a signed Isiah Thomas poster hanging in our living room, and he always wore this old Isiah Thomas jersey whenever he watched a Pistons game. I wonder where all that stuff is. I need to remember to ask Mama. The jersey might even fit me now.

I guess I'm thinking too hard, cuz Sneaky beats me in game three. It's cool being as loud as we want, with no Antwan to worry about, and no Charlie whining about not getting a turn.

"Game switch!" Sneaky says, grabbing *Star Wars Battlefront.* "You want some Oreos?"

"Yeah, where are they?"

"In the kitchen," Sneaky says. "Hold on, I'll be right back."

Sneaky tiptoes out, all stealth-mode, and I know he's probably gonna try to sneak some past his mom. After a few minutes, I hear Sneaky's footsteps coming down the hall, and a loud "SNEAKY!"

Sneaky tosses me the package of Oreos from the door and says, "Yeah?"

"Excuse me?" his mom calls from the living room.

"Yes, Mama?"

"What are you doing? Come here!"

Sneaky sighs and heads to the living room. I hear his mom fuss at him about playing video games all day, and I'm pretty sure she'll have us washing windows in a second. Sneaky says something, and then I don't hear anything else. A second later, Sneaky rushes into the room and closes the door.

"She 'bout to put us to work?" I ask.

"Nah, she got a phone call from some dude," Sneaky says, picking up his controller and turning the volume down a little.

"She got a boyfriend?"

"Nah, man," Sneaky says, twisting up his face. That means he's mad, and maybe what I just asked is true.

I don't say anything else. I'd probably be mad, too, if some guy was trying to hang around Mama.

We eat Oreos and play *Star Wars* for a long time, until Mama comes to pick me up. She talks with Sneaky's mom for a little while, which gives me and Sneaky a chance to practice our routine in front of Charlie. She tries to copy us, of course.

"If you let me dance with you guys, I know you'll win!" she begs. "I can do a flip; look!"

Charlie attempts a raggedy tumble that makes me and Sneaky bust up laughing.

"Maybe one day, Charlie," Sneaky says, patting her shoulder. Charlie runs to the living room to show off her flip to the adults.

"How long y'all gonna be staying in that motel?" Sneaky asks.

"I don't know," I tell Sneaky. "Till Mama gets more money, I guess."

"I hope y'all can get your old place," Sneaky says. "Then you can come over all the time, like before."

At first, that's what I hoped, too. But now I know our next place has to be better. We're gonna get a nice, big house. I'll hang the Isiah Thomas poster up in my room, and wear the Pistons jersey whenever Sneaky comes to visit.

May 9

FOR THE THIRD day in a row, I wake up to the sound of Mama humming and something sizzling. Yesterday it was pancakes, and today, it's real bacon! And even crazier, Mama's dressed up nice, like she's going somewhere special.

First thing I always do in the morning is check my backpack for Daddy's notebooks and the sock with my money. I do it every night, too. Once I see that everything's there, I walk over to where Mama's standing.

"Hey, Mama," I say. "You look nice."

"Thank you, baby," she says, flipping the strips of bacon. There's only four, and I'm hoping I get the extra piece.

"I think," begins Mama, spreading butter on slices of bread, "I think I'm ready to go back to work."

"For real?" I ask, feeling excited. If Mama starts working again, we'll be outta Smoky Inn in no time!

"Yes, for real," Mama says with a laugh. Then she stops what she's doing and gives me a hug.

"I miss Daddy so much," she says softly, her voice strong.

"I do, too," I say.

"This story thing would make him so proud, Isaiah," Mama says, finally letting me go. "Now I gotta make him proud, too."

While Charlie's still sleeping, me and Mama sit at the table and eat bread and bacon. She tells me that she's gonna meet with somebody at her old job, to see when she can start.

"You remember Ms. Martin, don't you, 'Saiah?" Mama asks.

"Um, yeah," I say, even though I don't.

"She told me to come back whenever I'm ready." Mama chews and swallows. "I think I'm ready."

I nod. This is the most me and her have talked in forever. I like it. I almost tell her about the money I'm saving, but nah. I think it'll be better to surprise her. Maybe when I have a little more.

We finish eating, and Mama goes to wake Charlie up, which means lots of whining is about to start. Charlie hates getting up early; always has. Usually, Mama lets her stay in her pajamas when they drop me off at school, but now she says Charlie's gonna have to go to daycare.

"Mommy, noooo!" Charlie groans, trying hard to keep the cover over her face.

"Charlie, there's bacon," I tell her, and she peeks out with a sleepy smile. Got her!

School is a breeze, probably because Mrs. Fisher's out, and the sub—this skinny dude with a ponytail—spends more time talking to us about his life than using the lesson notes I know Mrs. Fisher left. I hear a few girls whisper that he's soooo cute. Gross.

Having the sub makes it easy for me to get a pass and sneak to the lunchroom when the fourth graders are in there. Sneaky said he and Antwan went back to P.J.'s to buy more candy, and those guys from before weren't there. When I asked Sneaky why Antwan was being so nice to him, Sneaky said, "Everybody gonna be nice when you give them ten bucks!" He also said Antwan and his friends have beef with those other boys. The morning bell rang before I could ask him what kind of beef, but I know it can't be good.

I sell a bunch of candy during the fourth graders' lunch, which makes me even more hyped about going to the barbershop after school. I only work at the shop on Tuesdays and Thursdays, but I know I'm doing such an awesome job that pretty soon Rock's gonna want me there *every* day.

I hustle hard, and Rock gives me a whole twenty bucks for sweeping, mopping, and helping him restock hair supplies. I can't wait to put it in my sock. The money from today is gonna take me to seventy-four dollars! That plus Daddy's two-hundred-dollar prize money should have us out of Smoky Inn for good.

"You know how much apartments cost?" I ask Rock while I'm waiting for Mama to pick me up.

"It all depends, li'l man," Rock says. "How many rooms, if it's downtown or not, if it has a good view or not."

I think it would be pretty cool to have a place downtown, where you can look at the city lights at night.

"What about downtown?" I ask. "Three bedrooms."

Rock whistles. "That could be a nice chunk of change you talkin' about. Seventeen, eighteen hundred, maybe more."

Whoa. So maybe not downtown.

"Okay. What if it wasn't downtown?" I ask. "Just a regular place?"

"You shoppin' for real estate, li'l man?" Rock grins.

"No, it's something for school," I lie.

Rock tells me some places are six or seven hundred a month, which I figure could work for us if Mama gets her job back.

I'm putting the broom away when I hear Mama's horn beep loudly outside.

"Aight, 'Saiah," Rock says, nodding at me on my way out. "See ya Thursday."

I tell Rock bye and run to the car.

"Hey, Mama. Hey, Charlie," I say. I put my fingers in my pocket and feel the crinkle of the crisp twenty. Mama says hey, but she leans forward with a frown to look into New Growth.

"'Saiah, I don't know about this," she says. "What boy needs to be hanging around a barbershop with crazy grown men?"

I want to ask her about being left at the library all day, which happens all the time. At least I'm making money at the barbershop.

Which reminds me . . .

"Mama, how was work?"

Mama ignores my question.

"Boy, did you hear me ask you about this barbershop? I'm grown; I don't need you askin' about my day."

"But, Mama, you met Rock already, remember? He cuts Sneaky's hair and his wife does Miz Rita's hair."

Mama doesn't seem convinced. I notice that she doesn't have on the same nice clothes she had on before. Now she's wearing her faded gray sweats.

She mumbles something as she drives off. It's like she forgot all about her talk with Rock, how he told her it would be cool to have me helping around the shop.

"Mommy didn't get her job back," Charlie says before sticking two fingers in her mouth.

Aww, man . . .

"Charlie!" Mama says, but not in a real mad voice. She looks at me in the rearview mirror. My eyes ask her what happened, because my mouth can't. She sighs.

"I guess I waited too long," Mama tells me. "They filled my position."

Aww, man . . .

"I thought they said—"

"Yeah," Mama says, "I thought they said that, too."

My face must be real upset, because Mama calls my name in a way that makes me look up.

"Isaiah, don't even worry. It's all gonna work out. I'm gonna find something better."

I don't say anything. I open my backpack, check for the sock. Then I grab Daddy's notebook and hope I can find something inside to help me know what to do next.

May 12

THERE'S A BOTTLE in the trash can in 109.

I hear the *clink* sound when I go to throw away the empty can of beans we had for dinner last night. I stare at the trash can for a minute. Maybe I imagined the sound, or maybe it's something else, like the can of beans from dinner the night before last. I glare at the bathroom door, where Mama's taking a shower. Charlie's dressed, but she's under the covers trying to sleep. I reach into the trash.

I feel like when me and Sneaky were wrestling and he accidentally elbowed me in the stomach, hard.

The bottle is cool and smooth in my hand and I want to fling it at the wall and watch it explode into a million pieces.

"What's that?"

Charlie's voice makes me jump. I drop the bottle into the trash and whirl around.

"Back up!" I say. "You can't be creeping up on me like that!"

"I'm not!" Charlie says. She tries to peek into the trash, but I push her back toward her and Mama's bed.

"I'm telling! You pushed me!" Charlie yells.

"So? You get on my nerves!"

Charlie and I scowl at each other. The phone rings, and she bounces to it before I can stop her. Mama told us to never answer that phone, and to only use it if there's an emergency.

"Charlie, don't—"

"Hello?" Charlie picks up the phone. "No, she's in the—"

I snatch the phone from Charlie, and she sticks out her tongue at me.

"Hello?" says the voice on the other end, sounding upset. "Is Lisa Dunn available?"

"Um, no, she's not available right now."

The voice sighs. "Well, we need her to call the main office right away. Can you tell her that?"

"Yeah, I can tell her," I say, my heart thumping.

"Thank you." *Click.*

Mama comes from the bathroom, and her face is a cloud. I'm pretty sure the person on the phone was only bringing rain. So I don't say a word about the call. Not today.

When Mama drops me off at school, I climb from the car without saying goodbye.

"'Sup, Isaiah?" says Sneaky when I sit down across from him in the lunchroom for breakfast.

"Hey," I say. I stab a Tater Tot with my fork, and I can barely taste it when I pop it into my mouth.

"Check the kicks." Sneaky grins, sliding his foot out from under the table. "Got 'em yesterday."

I stare at his shoes, and for some reason, seeing them just makes me even madder. Sneaky's my best friend and all, but right now I feel like dumping a spoonful of ketchup on his brand-new shoes.

"Nice," I say, not really caring about his stupid shoes.

"What's wrong with you?" Sneaky asks.

"Nothing." I dunk my French toast sticks in the little tub of syrup. Sneaky likes his plain, but he always gets an extra syrup for me. He tosses it to me like always, but it bumps the one I already have and spills on my tray.

"Watch it!" I yell, louder than I mean to.

"Dang, chill out, bro!" Sneaky says, giving me a look. "It was an accident. Why you trippin'?"

I stand up without giving Sneaky an answer. I'm not hungry anymore, so I pick up my tray and toss everything in the trash. And even though it's stupid, I don't talk to Sneaky for the rest of the day.

May 15

"HEY, STRANGER!" MR. Shephard holds out his fist when I walk into the children's section.

"Hey, Mr. Shephard," I say, bumping my fist to his.

"How you been?" he asks.

"Okay," I say. I tell him about my job at the barbershop.

"Nice," he says. "You saving for something special?"

"I don't know." I shrug. Mr. Shephard nods. He's cool, but I know I can't be telling him that me and Mama and Charlie are staying in a motel. Or that Mama's the reason we're still there. Or that things are kinda weird between me and Sneaky. We met up over the weekend for one last practice before the talent show, but it didn't feel the same. We probably won't win unless we can get back to normal. But how is that supposed to happen?

I head over to my special table by the window and drop my backpack on it.

"So what're you reading today?" Mr. Shephard asks.

"Nothin'." I shrug. I don't tell Mr. Shephard I'm gonna try to write something of my own today.

The whole poetry project got me into reading Langston Hughes poems, so when Mr. Shephard walks by again, I ask if he's ever heard of him.

"Yep, sure have," Mr. Shephard says. "You got good taste. Wanna grab a book about him?"

"Okay," I say. Me and Mr. Shephard go to the computer first, and he shows me how to type in Langston Hughes's name and pick which books I want to find.

"That one's gonna be over in the biography section, and those are in fiction." Mr. Shephard points me in the right direction. Some older kids come into the children's section making noise, so he goes over to tell them to chill. I find *Poetry for Young People: Langston Hughes,* and another book about his life, then head over to my table and start reading.

"What's that?"

A backpack plops on my table, and I look up and see Angel staring down at my book. Too late to try to hide it, I guess.

"A book about Langston Hughes," I say, like it's no big deal.

"For school?" she asks.

"No."

"So you just like it?" Angel's face is twisted up like she's 'bout to laugh, but I don't even care.

"Yeah, I like it," I tell her loudly, daring her to say something.

Angel shrugs and sits down across from me. She unzips her backpack (pink) and pulls out her pink notebook. After flipping through it, she spins it around and points to a page.

"This is my favorite one by him," Angel says. I read her bubbly writing of a poem called "I, Too."

"My granddaddy made us memorize that one when we were really little," Angel tells me. "He was always reciting it for no reason. Once, I said the whole thing when I got sent from the table for playing with my food."

"What happened?" I ask, imagining Angel saying the poem with an attitude.

"Everybody busted up laughing," Angel says. This time there's an actual smile on her face. "I didn't get in trouble."

I grin, too. "So you make up poems?" I ask. Never thought Angel would like the same thing as me. I mean, we worked on the poetry project and all, but she never said she wrote poems.

"Um, no." Angel flips through her notebook some more so I can see. "I write down poems I like. I'm not some kinda weird rhyming genius like you."

I like that. Maybe I'm Isaiah Dunn, Rhyming Genius. Bet Daddy would've written some cool stories about that.

"So how come you can make up poems right off the top of your head?" Angel asks.

"I dunno." I shrug. "It's easy to me, I guess."

I'm about to tell Angel about how the words fist-fight to get out of my head when her eyes drift away to something over my shoulder, and her eyebrows bunch up.

"Hey, ain't that your mama?"

I turn and see Mama come into the children's area, and right away I know something's not right.

Mama's wobbling as she walks, and when she says hello to Mr. Shephard, her voice is loud—too loud for the library. Charlie trails behind her, her eyes big and scared. When she sees me, she races past Mama and grips my arm.

"C'mon, Isaiah, let's go!" Mama calls. I'm already up and grabbing my bag.

"Bye," Angel says.

I don't say anything back.

One of the loud kids snickers when I pass their table, and I glare at him. I recognize him from school, and even though he whispers, I still hear what he says about Mama.

"Isaiah, did you want to check those out?" Mr. Shephard asks, nodding at the Langston Hughes books I'm still holding.

"Um, no," I say, handing him the books. "Maybe later."

Right now, we have to leave. Fast!

"I shouldn't have to come inside looking for you, Isaiah,"

Mama says loudly. I see heads turn as we walk through the main part of the library.

Almost to the door. Almost to the door.

Mama bumps a cart of books, and I reach for her arm to steady her. She snatches it away. Somehow we make it to the car, where Mama fumbles with the keys for a few seconds.

After she finally gets it open, I climb in after Charlie. She scoots her booster seat to the middle, close to me, and doesn't let go of my arm.

"Hey, Charlie, you gotta let go for a second," I say, trying to put on my seat belt with one hand. It doesn't go too well, and I have to pull away from her to do it. Mama starts the car.

"Should you even be driving?"

I thought the words were just in my head, but nope, they actually flew from my mouth.

"What?" Mama turns around to face me. I stare at my shoes. Mama mumbles something and keeps driving. I pray like crazy that she doesn't crash us into something. I don't notice that I'm squeezing Charlie's hand until she says, "Ow!"

"Sorry," I tell her.

We get to the motel in one piece, and as soon as we walk inside 109 and shut the door, Mama plops onto the bed. I help Charlie wash up and put on her pj's, and then I put on mine. Before I turn off all the lights, I reach in my backpack for my notebook. The words in my head gotta come out or I won't be able to sleep.

But I don't get to write a single word. Everything just gets worse when I reach inside, and a million times worse when I dump everything onto the floor.

Daddy's sock is gone.

May 16

THE POUNDING ON the door makes me jump. I'm sitting on the couch, writing a list in Daddy's notebook. The list is every place I've been with my backpack, and where the money could've gotten stolen. My first thought is school, but my bag is always, *always* locked up in my locker. Plus, I already checked in the office today, and no one turned in any money. At the barbershop after school, it was the same thing. No missing money. Rock wished me luck on trying to find the cash, but I'm not having any luck at all.

Bam! Bam! Bam!

Mama stares at the door; she looks surprised, too. Nobody knows we're here, so nobody's ever come to see us. I get up to go to the door, but Mama beats me to it. She peeks in the peephole, then just stands still. There's another pound, and Mama jumps a tiny bit before unlocking the door.

Two guys. One is the always-angry guy from the main office. The other is a cop.

The cop looks at Mama and nods slightly. The guy from the office stares at everything except Mama's face.

"Ma'am? Sleep Inn management notified us that you have not made a payment in three weeks, despite repeated attempts to collect. I'll have to escort you off the premises if you are unable to make payment at this time."

Mama doesn't say anything. Her face isn't shocked like mine is, and that makes the karate-chopping start up in my stomach. Especially when she turns to me with eyes that are blank.

"Isaiah, you and Charlie go get your stuff."

I stare at Mama, then Charlie, who's sucking her fingers and watching TV, then back to Mama. For some reason, my feet can't move and my mouth can't talk.

"We'll give you a few moments to gather your belongings," says the guy from the office. He doesn't sound as mean as before, but he doesn't say, "Hey, I'll give you a few extra days," either. They both leave the doorway, but they don't go far away.

"Charlie," Mama says, staring past me, "make sure all your toys and clothes are in your basket."

Mama walks to the small kitchen area and grabs the few pots, pans, and bowls that we have. She moves like a robot, like she's blocking out everything except the next thing she's about to grab.

"Isaiah, get your stuff together. We have to go."

Normally I would be doing what she said. But I swear, I can't move a muscle.

"Mama—" I finally say, but she cuts me off by slamming a bowl on the counter.

"Just do it, Isaiah! Charlise, *now*!"

"Mama, why don't you just give them the money from the contest?"

Mama's not facing me, so I don't see her face. But her shoulders drop just a tiny bit. And I know.

She doesn't have that money anymore. And I don't have *my* money anymore, or I could've saved us. I could've been like the superhero Daddy wrote about. But I'm not.

I start slamming clothes into my basket, and I have to keep blinking because my eyes feel all prickly with the tears trying to stab their way out. I get my toothbrush from the bathroom, and make sure Daddy's notebook is in my backpack. I don't care about anything else.

Charlie's quiet as she puts her dolls and clothes into her basket. I wonder what she's thinking, why she's not screaming and crying like a baby, the way I want to. Mama carries the kitchen things to the car, and I don't help at all. Takes her three trips. She puts the bathroom stuff in garbage bags and carries that by herself, too.

In less than an hour, the stupid room is emptied of all our

things. Mama walks around, making sure we're not leaving anything behind. When she turns off the TV and opens her mouth to say something to me and Charlie, I sling my backpack over my shoulder, yank up my basket, and brush past her to the door.

"Hey, kid." The office guy nods over at me. "You guys have somewhere to go?"

"Yeah," I tell him. "Somewhere new."

"That's good." He nods again, spits in the grass. When Mama walks toward us he says, "I don't like doing this, y'know. But this is a business, and we have to collect payment. . . ."

Mama glares at him, and his voice trails off.

"Ma'am, could I speak with you over here?" asks the cop.

"Yes," Mama snaps. "If I can get my babies in the car."

She opens the door, and Charlie climbs in and buckles up. I toss my basket in the trunk and get in beside Charlie.

"Stay in the car," Mama tells us before walking over to the cop. He does some talking, and Mama nods and points off to somewhere in the distance. I wish I knew what she's saying. Probably how we're gonna go stay with a cousin or grandparent or best friend or something. Or how we have this nice new place that's finally ready. Three bathrooms and a playroom, just like we talked about.

When Mama comes back to the car, she slams her door, starts the engine, and speeds toward the exit, right in front of the cop.

"Where we going now, Mama?" Charlie asks, staring out her window at Smoky Inn.

"I don't know," Mama says. At least she's honest.

Someone in a car nearby is blasting Bruno Mars, and it's right then that I remember tonight is the talent show. My heart sinks even more. No way can I ask Mama to drop me off at school, or even call Sneaky to tell him what happened. One minute I'm trying to figure out where my money could be, and the next minute, the cop was pounding on the door and everything else faded from my mind.

We exit the parking lot of the motel, and as much as I hated the place, right now, I think I'm hating Mama more.

May 17

I CRASH INTO morning with a sore neck and an empty stomach. I keep my eyes squeezed shut, cuz when I open them, I'll know it wasn't all just a nightmare.

Charlie kicks me in the butt, literally, and I officially wake up. First thing I see is Mama's seat, reclined way back, close to my face. I stare at a stain on the seat and try to remember what it came from. Maybe an ice cream cone, or ketchup from French fries. It's a stupid stain, but I feel like I have to know. I sit up and rub the sleep from my eyes. I really, really have to use the bathroom.

My stomach growls, and before I can stop it, I let out a huge fart.

"Oh Lord," Mama mutters a few seconds later when the funk hits her. I smile, even though I don't want to.

Mama scoots her chair forward and cracks the window. A blast of cold air fills the car, and I pull my hoodie/blanket close to my chin. Charlie's the only one with a real blanket, and she's bundled up like a caterpillar, except for the leg that kicked me.

Mama sighs, and I swallow up the words I was about to say—that I'm starving. Mama starts the car, looks at me in the rear-view mirror.

"Seat belt, 'Saiah," she says. I buckle up and glance over at Charlie.

"Want me to wake her up?"

Mama thinks for a second, and shakes her head.

"We're not going far," she tells me.

And she's right. A few turns later and we're in front of Woodson Elementary.

My school.

I sit very still, but my heart is thumping and my stomach feels like there's a tennis match going on inside of it.

"It's a little early," Mama says, "but you'll be able to use the bathroom and get breakfast."

I still don't move. Mama can't be serious. It's gotta be April

Fools' all over again. But I know she's for real when she turns around to look at me. She opens her mouth, and my nose crinkles when I smell her breath. Mine must be just as bad. She's saying something about washing my face and swishing some water around in my mouth, but her words sound muffled, like I'm inside a giant bubble. I nod when I'm supposed to.

"'Saiah, I know this isn't—wasn't—the best night. But we're okay. We're gonna be okay. It'll be much better when I pick you up, okay?"

I feel better when she says that.

But I don't believe her.

The school is pretty quiet when I go inside. Guess this is how it is before all the kids get here. I trudge to the bathroom and do what Mama says: swish water in my mouth and wash my face with a cold paper towel.

"Hey, Isaiah, you're here early." Ms. Marlee waves at me as I walk down the hallway to the lunchroom.

"Yeah, um, my mom got a new job and, um, she had to drop me early," I say. I don't know why I say the lie; it just comes out.

"Oh, good for her!" Ms. Marlee says, and I can tell she really means it. "And I'm really proud of your work in the ReStore program. I'd love to have you be a peer mentor next year; you *and* Angel."

"Thanks," I tell Ms. Marlee. I don't know if I wanna be a

mentor, but for Ms. Marlee, I'll definitely think about it. I wonder if Ms. Marlee already mentioned it to Angel, and if she's thinking about it, too.

The action in the hallway picks up as the buses get here, but I'm still first in line for breakfast.

"Can I get two?" I ask, my stomach grumbling as I stare at the mini cinnamon rolls. The lunch lady pauses, and I think she's gonna say no, but then she puts an extra roll on my plate and winks.

I sit down at a table by myself and am done by the time I see Sneaky jump in line for his breakfast. My stomach drops when I think about missing the talent show, and I stand up quick to dump my tray. I don't get there in time, though, cuz Sneaky sees me, and he doesn't look happy.

"Yo, Isaiah, where were you yesterday?" he asks, glaring at me.

"Nowhere," I say.

"Serious, man? You left me hangin' at the talent show."

"So?" I say, mad at Sneaky for getting mad at me. "It wasn't my fault."

I want to ask him if he still did the dance, but I'm guessing he didn't. A part of me doesn't even care. At least he has a home to go to, *and* fresh Jordans on his feet.

"Whatever, man," Sneaky says. He shakes his head like I'm the worst disappointment ever.

"The dance was stupid anyway," I say.

"Oh yeah?" Sneaky's eyes narrow. "Well, I guess my candy business is stupid, too. You can find your own hustle."

"I already did!" I say, but Sneaky's walking away. Ignoring me. His best friend.

I throw everything in the trash can, including the tray. I kick the trash can, too.

"Dang, calm down! You and the trash can 'bout to be in the ReStore room with Ms. Marlee."

I turn and see Angel with a smug look on her face.

"Whatever," I say.

" 'Whatever,' " she says, copying how I sound. "What's up with Sneaky?"

"Nothin'."

"I just heard you guys," Angel says. "He's actin' dumb."

"So?"

"Soooo, I have an idea," Angel says. "For your new hustle. Meet at the library after school?"

"What's the idea?" I ask.

"Library. After school." Angel dumps her tray and walks away without saying anything else.

I have no idea what Mama's doing right now, or if she'll have a place for us to sleep by the end of the day. But I do know I'll be at the library after school. No matter what.

May 18

we stopped
Being friends
As fast as
Popsicles melt
Outside on a blazing hot day
And drip down your fingers
Like tears.

May 20

Things I learned about Angel:

1. She likes Beyoncé. A lot.
2. She has crazy ideas, but sometimes they're also good.
3. She has a dad, but he's not very nice to her mom.
4. Her favorite food is pizza. She *maybe* coulda beat me at
   the pizza-eating contest.

For Angel's idea, I write in Daddy's notebook every chance I get, putting my words in the white spaces near his. I'm not sure it'll work, but at least we're giving it a try. Angel says today will just be "practice," but I'm still nervous.

"You got the paper and pens?" I ask her when I get to the front of the library.

"You're late," she says, staring at her pink watch.

"Not really," I tell her, even though I am. Last night was our fourth time sleeping in the car, and it's not fun at all. Mama got us day passes to the YMCA so we could swim and use the showers, but instead of staying there with her and Charlie, I begged to come to the library. Ran all the way over.

"Whatever," Angel says. She puts a hat on one of the library steps and points to the step above it. "Stand right there, okay?"

She's bossy, but I do what she says. Angel puts a few dollars in the hat, and I drop in a handful of change, just like we talked about. It's supposed to be a trigger to people of what they need to do. She sits a step above me and gets out a bright yellow sheet of paper. She starts cutting it with these fancy scissors and arranges her pens next to her.

"Okay, these two coming right now," she whispers to me. I look and see an older couple walking from the parking lot holding hands. The guy has a bag of books in his other hand, and the lady is smiling for no reason. They must be in love.

"Something about love, okay?" Angel hisses, grabbing a red pen.

"Got it," I whisper back. I close my eyes and touch Daddy's notebook, which is right beside me. When the couple gets close, I say:

"Love is like the sun,
Big, and warm, and bright.
You know it's always there,
Just sometimes out of sight.
Love comes to the library,
And love checks out a book.
Love takes out the trash,
And love will learn to cook.
We need love more than we know,
So plant a seed, and let love grow."

"Oh my!" The lady stops in her tracks and puts a hand over her mouth for a second. "That was lovely, young man!"

"Thank you," I say. And like Angel told me, I say something else to "engage" them. "How are you guys today?"

"Just fine," says the guy, giving me a smile. "And how are you? Busy with your poems, I see."

"Yes," I say. "Just something I like doing."

"Would you like a copy of the poem?" Angel asks, holding up the yellow sheet. Man, she writes fast! And neat. She's got my words in red bubble letters.

"Well, uh . . ." The guy looks like he wants to pull his wife inside, but she's not having it.

"That would be wonderful, young lady!"

She goes digging in her purse, and Angel says, "Oh, we don't charge, ma'am. We are a donation-based business."

I hold my breath.

"Oh." The lady looks a little confused until she sees the hat, the one we put money in. "Well, isn't that the smartest thing, Harold?"

The lady chuckles and drops a few dollars into the hat.

"Keep it up, young people; that was very nice," she says. "I'll put this on my fridge!"

When the couple goes inside, Angel grins and nudges me.

"See! Told ya!" she says. "If Justin Bieber could blow up by sitting out there singing to people, you can make some money saying poems to people. 'Specially since you can do it on the spot like that."

I can't stop smiling, especially when I look in the hat and see what the lady put in.

"It's a five wrapped up in a one!" I tell Angel.

"Uh-huh!" Angel's all grins, too. She grabs another sheet of paper and starts cutting. "Make sure you ready for the next one!"

We stay outside for another hour, me saying poems and Angel writing them all fancy. Not everybody stops, and not everybody throws cash into our hat, but it's still fun, and I don't have to sneak around selling candy to do it.

"When you get really good, we can have Jules record you and put it on YouTube," says Angel.

"YouTube?"

"Yeah," Angel says, like it's a no-brainer. "That's how Justin and Shawn Mendes did it, right?"

"I guess." I shrug. I'm not really trying to be like either of those guys, but if that'll get us into a real house, YouTube, here I come!

I'm a mix of sad and mad when I see Mama pull up. I don't tell Angel that the car is also our house, and that I'll say poems all day and night if it means I don't have to sleep crammed in the backseat with Charlie or use baby wipes to wash up. That's the kind of stuff I would only tell Sneaky, if we were talking. I just tell Angel I'll see her at school. The way she tells me bye makes me think she already understands. And when I'm in the car, I know for sure, cuz I find a piece of paper mixed in with the money we split. Only two words, written in bubbly pink letters:

I'M SORRY.

May 22

"MAMA, WHERE'S CHARLIE?"

We've been driving around for almost an hour, and Mama keeps making weird turns, swerving, and muttering to herself. Today's a half day, and I was shocked when Mama picked me up on time. Sorta. She was actually a little early. I was worried when the office called my name to get picked up during science, and when I didn't see Charlie in the car, I felt even worse. I know that Mama put Charlie in a free preschool, but she only goes for half a day, and now the clock in the car says 1:07.

I missed lunch, so my stomach is rumbling. Too bad I'm not in the candy business anymore; I would've probably had a Snickers or something in my backpack. Not being friends with Sneaky is gonna take forever to get used to.

I'm about to ask about Charlie again when I hear the buzz of Mama's phone ringing. I lean forward and see it on the front seat, with the name "Rita Sanders" flashing across the screen.

"Mama, is Charlie with Miz Rita?" I ask. "Miz Rita's calling you right now."

Mama ignores her phone. It stops ringing, then starts back up a few seconds later. Miz Rita again. I reach for the phone myself, thinking that maybe something happened to Charlie, but Mama grabs it and says "Hello?" super loud.

Mama goes, "Uh-huh. Uh-huh. And why they call you? *I'm* the mother!"

I can't hear a thing Miz Rita's saying, plus my heart is beating extra loud and fast. Mama hangs up the phone and tosses it onto the seat.

"Mama, is Charlie okay?" I ask, my voice all high like a little kid.

"Yeah, she's fine," Mama snaps. "We're gonna get her."

I sit back hard against the seat. And then, for some stupid reason, tears start falling from my eyes. I wipe them away fast, and tell myself that everything's okay. But really, I'm tired of telling myself that.

We pull up to Charlie's daycare, and she's walking out with a big smile, holding Miz Rita's hand. Mama runs onto the curb a little and jumps from the car before I'm even sure it's parked.

Mama starts yelling at Miz Rita, and I get out to try to stop her. Miz Rita's face is calm and firm, like she knows what she's getting into, the kind of storm Mama is.

"Isaiah, get back in that car!" yells Mama.

Charlie's smile disappears.

"What's wrong, Mama?" she asks.

"Charlie, c'mon," I say, reaching for her hand. She sees my tears and starts crying herself. I feel like the worst hero ever.

"Isaiah baby, you and Charlie go wait in the car," Miz Rita says. She gives me a quick squeeze. "It's gonna be okay, baby. Let me talk to your mama."

I pull Charlie to the car, and she keeps turning around to see Mama, who's still yelling. A few people walking by point and stare, and I wish we had magic beans and rice to make us disappear.

"What's wrong with Mama?" Charlie asks me in the car. "Is she gonna die?"

"No, Charlie!" I say quickly. "She's okay."

But as I watch Miz Rita trying to reach for Mama, and Mama snatching away, I realize that she does *not* look okay.

Miz Rita's talking soft, so I don't hear what she's saying. But I hear Mama say, "It's our anniversary! It's our anniversary, and he's not here!" Mama's crying hard now, and finally, she falls into Miz Rita's arms.

May 23

I'VE WOKEN UP in this building thousands of times—in my old place or Sneaky's. But when I wake up in Miz Rita's apartment, it feels weird, and not right. The room I'm in is pitch black and quiet, except for a clock that's tick, tick, ticking away. No Charlie snoring, no Mama moving around. I can't sleep.

I sit up and blink until I can see good enough to get out of bed and walk to the door. A tiny bit of light hits my face when I open it, and I hear soft voices coming from the kitchen. I tiptoe down the hall, and luckily, Miz Rita's floor's not squeaky like ours was. I pass Charlie knocked out on the couch, but no Mama.

I peek into the kitchen and see Mama and Miz Rita sitting at the table. Crumpled tissues cover the table like snow, and both Mama and Miz Rita have their hands wrapped around two mugs with steam coming out of them. Mama's head is down, so she doesn't see me, and Miz Rita's sitting sideways, looking at Mama, so she doesn't see me, either.

"I just don't see how I can go on," Mama says. "Some days I don't even want to."

"I know, sweetie, I know," Miz Rita says. I yank my head back when Mama looks up to grab another tissue from the box on the table.

"I should be out of tears by now," Mama says. That makes me think about writing a poem, one about tears. Miz Rita says something nice to Mama, but I don't really hear her. I'm too busy thinking about my words. I wonder if Daddy did the same thing. Maybe while he was working, he thought about his stories. I ninja-walk back down the hall, close the door, and turn on the light. I open my notebook to a free space and write:

> I should be out of tears, but more keep falling.
> where they coming from? I can't stop bawling.
> where do tears start? where do they end?
> I wish they'd stop soon, and never come again.

When I'm done writing, I close the notebook and put it next to Daddy's in my backpack. Then I turn off the light and tiptoe back down the hall. When I get to Charlie, I scoot her over on the couch and climb under the blanket with her. She doesn't even move. I listen to her breathing, and to Miz Rita and Mama in the kitchen, until I can't keep my eyes and ears open anymore.

May 24

MIZ RITA MAKES breakfast like Sneaky's mom does: giant biscuits, grits, eggs, and sausages. I eat till my stomach hurts and I wanna lay down and watch cartoons. But nope, that's not what happens next.

"Isaiah, need you to take this garbage to the trash room," Miz Rita says. She's already got Charlie taking dishes to the sink, so I know there's no way out of it.

"Okay," I say, grabbing the two bags. Before I go, I notice that Miz Rita's fixing a separate plate.

"This is for your Mama," she tells me. "She's resting, but she'll be hungry when she gets up."

Mama's been resting a whole lot. Crying, too. But there are no bottles clinking around in the garbage bags I'm carrying, so I guess things are better.

I walk down the hall to the trash room, which pretty much smells like a dirty toilet. As I'm tossing the bags into the huge bin, an old lady comes hobbling in with her trash bags.

"Sweet Jesus, that's a stink!" she says, wrinkling up her face. "Baby, can you toss these bags in there for me?"

I do what she asks, and she turns to go, then stops right outside the door and studies me.

"Baby, you know the elevator's broke again—ain't surprised—but my friend up on the eighth floor can't be carryin' all them bags down the steps, old as she is. Would you mind toting her bags down for her?"

Aww, man! Miz Rita probably set me up and told all her old lady friends I'm staying with her so they can give me work to do.

"Okay," I tell the old lady, and she grins. She pulls a cell phone from her pocket and frowns as she tries to unlock the screen.

"Now what he say my password was?" she mutters, tapping away until she figures out the right combination. "Ha! Got it!"

Man, I wish Sneaky was here right now. We'd be cracking up!

If we were still friends.

"Hello, Ida?" the old lady speaks loudly into her phone, and her friend is just as loud. "Ida! I got somebody comin' to take your garbage, all right? His name is—what's your name, baby?"

"Isaiah."

"Oooh, Lawd, he got a good name, Ida. His name's Isaiah, and he's a handsome fella." There's a pause, and I hear her friend ask if I got my pants pulled up. The old lady studies me. "He got on shorts. Anyway, he comin' now."

She ends her call abruptly and puts the phone back in her pocket.

"Go on up to 806, baby," she says, patting my arm. "You a nice boy."

I run up the stairs to the eighth floor and knock on 806. After a few seconds, the door opens with the chain still on.

"Who's that?"

"Isaiah," I say, seeing half of the lady's face. I guess she's Miz Ida.

She closes the door, and I hear her taking the chain off. When she opens the door again, I see that she looks a lot like the first old lady.

"Good morning, Isaiah," she says. Her face ain't as smiley as the first lady's.

"Good morning," I say. "The lady said you needed me to take your trash down."

"Yes. My friend Annie is always meddlin' in my business," says Miz Ida, opening the door wider to show two garbage bags sitting there. "But she's right; it'd take me all day to get these down to that garbage room and back. I 'preciate your help."

"You're welcome," I tell her, grabbing the two bags. Before she closes the door, though, I think about what Angel would do right now.

"'Scuse me," I say. "Do you want to buy a poem?"

"A poem?" Miz Ida squints at me like I must be joking.

"Yeah, I write poems," I tell her. "My friend puts them on fancy paper and we sell them."

I recite my poem about how me and Sneaky aren't friends anymore, and the one about summertime. Miz Ida looks shocked.

"Well, if I ain't seen everything," she says, shaking her head. "Tell you what; you come back next week to get my garbage again, and I'll buy a poem."

"Yes, ma'am!" I say. "What do you want the poem to be about?"

"Broken elevators," she says, shaking her head. "Write somethin' about that!"

"Okaaay," I say, grabbing her garbage bags.

"Hold on, now, baby," Miz Ida says, holding out two crisp dollars. "For your time. I'll see you next week, all right?"

I nod and put the money in my pocket.

"See you next week."

"I'll be ready for my poem."

It might take me all week to come up with something good, but I'll be ready, too.

May 25

MIZ RITA AND Mama don't know I heard them talking.

Charlie's taking a bubble bath even though it's mad early, and I'm supposed to be studying vocabulary words, but my stomach starts rumbling, so I get up to grab an apple or something from the kitchen. I also wanna see if they'll let me go to the barbershop today, like I'm supposed to. I stop at the door when Miz Rita says, "It'll be just fine, Lisa. With Shayna headin' off to college, Charlie can have her room. Long as he don't mind, Isaiah can stay in my sewing room."

Shayna's Miz Rita's daughter—well, granddaughter, really, but she calls Miz Rita "Ma." Charlie sticks to Shayna like glue, so she'll probably love to sleep in her room.

Mama says something soft that I can't hear all the way, and then Miz Rita says, "But you need to. For *you*."

That's when Charlie pops up behind me and says "Hey, Isaiah!" mad loud. Things get quiet in the kitchen, and then I hear the chairs scrape against the floor, and the clanking of pots and pans. Ugh! I groan and push past Charlie down the hall to where I've been sleeping, in Miz Rita's sewing room. There's a sewing machine in the corner and this mannequin thing that freaked me out the first few nights, because it looks like a person in the dark, especially with the huge hat Miz Rita has on its head. She told me she could move it out or cover it up if it scared me, but I said I was okay.

I take Daddy's advice again, but this time, I don't write my fear down. I give it a real name. Daddy said if we ever got a dog, he'd want to name it Ink, which makes sense now that I know he was a writer. So I'm thinking about naming the mannequin Ink. But it's definitely a girl, with curves and boobies and everything, so I name it Inka instead. Inka, the statue lady.

"'Sup, Inka?" I say, nodding at her. She really doesn't have eyes, but it looks like she's staring at me. "Yo, you're pretty creepy."

Inka doesn't say anything, of course, but she still gives me an idea. I take out my notebook and write, *Inka, the secret Keeper.* In my mind, I imagine Inka being some statue princess that no one pays attention to, but what they don't know is that she holds the secrets of all who talk around her. Not just secrets, but codes and clues and stuff, too. I wonder what it would be like to write a whole story like Daddy did. Maybe I'll try it one day. For now, I stay busy coming up with new poems to sell. I write words until Charlie bounces in to tell me it's time for dinner. So much for the barbershop.

"How's the homework comin', Isaiah?" Miz Rita asks me.

"Good," I say. I look from her to Mama and remember what they were talking about before. Then it hits me. They were talking about rooms and everything, but nobody said where Mama's gonna sleep.

May 26

"I GOTTA TELL you something."

Me and Angel are working on poem stuff at the playground by Miz Rita's place. It's the same playground me and Sneaky used to shoot baskets at, so I'm already feeling a little down by being here. The way Angel's looking right now doesn't make me feel any better.

"You know that day at the library, when your mom came in?"

"Yeah," I say. "So?"

"I think I know who stole your money," Angel says. She looks at me, then down at her shoes, and I know she isn't lying.

I wanna ask so many questions, but my mouth isn't saying a thing.

"Alex is my cousin," Angel says; then she corrects herself. "Well, like my third cousin, really. And he was runnin' his mouth about how him and his dumb friends jacked somebody's money at the library. When you told me what happened to your candy money, I kinda put it all together."

I don't even know Alex; at least I don't think I do. But I remember a group of kids being loud while Mr. Shephard and I looked at Langston Hughes books. And I remember that I left my backpack on the table. For only a second.

"When he told me, I got mad," Angel says. "I punched him and got in trouble."

"For real?" I ask. I can see her doing something like that. Makes me feel better. But not eighty-three dollars and sixty-two cents better.

"Yeah," Angel says. "That was messed up! Who steals at the library?"

"I guess Alex does," I say. I wonder if he still has my money.

"He spent the money on some stupid video game," Angel says, reading my mind. Crazy! "I should break it next time I'm over there!"

"Yeah, you should," I say. But I don't want Angel to get in trouble. I need her handwriting.

I let Angel read the poem I came up with for Miz Ida. I called it "Broke Up, Broke Down," and I think it's kinda funny. Angel does, too, cuz she's laughing by the time she's finished.

"Okay, how 'bout @Dunn Poems?" Angel asks. "Get it? The @ is for Atkins; your last name is Dunn." We've been trying to come up with an official name for our business, and I think this is the best one so far.

"Get @ us for a poem that's Dunn right!" I say.

"See, perfect!" Angel gives me dap, and we start drawing logo ideas. The sound of a basketball bouncing makes us both look up.

"Uh-oh," Angel says. Sneaky's coming into the playground area, and he's not alone.

Four guys saunter in with him, and from the angry look on Angel's face, one of them is probably Alex. Why would Sneaky hang with dudes who stole from me? Does he know? Sneaky acts like nothing's wrong at all; he's laughing and joking with these guys the same way he used to with me. He freezes for a second when he sees me and Angel.

"Hold up," I hear him tell the guys, and he starts walking over to us.

"Hey," Sneaky says when he gets close enough.

"Hey," I say.

"What're y'all doing?" he asks, nodding toward the paper and my notebook.

"A project," I say at the same time Angel says, "Our business."

"Oh, for real?" Sneaky has a smirk on his face, but he also seems a little hurt.

"Yeah."

"Aight, then," Sneaky says, turning back toward his new friends. "Catch you later."

"Yeah," I say again. Then I add, "We're staying with Miz Rita for a little bit."

One of the dudes calls for Sneaky to come on, but he looks back at me.

"For real?"

"Yeah."

Sneaky doesn't say anything else, but I can tell exactly what he *wants* to say.

Wish you could come by sometime.

I don't say anything, either, but I'm sure he can tell what *I* want to say.

Me too.

May 27

"COP A SQUAT, Isaiah."

"Huh?"

It's Saturday, but the barbershop was so busy, Rock asked me to come in.

I'm sweeping up hair when Rock pats the chair where he just finished hooking somebody's fade.

"C'mon and sit down, li'l man," Rock says. "Time for me to do some magic on that head."

Dang, is my hair that bad? It's probably been over a month since my last cut, and the barber wasn't that great. I'm glad the shop has cleared out from earlier; nobody here to clown me. I put the broom to the side and sheepishly walk over to Rock.

"If you ain't notice," says Rock, "everybody here leaves on point. That goes for you, too, li'l man."

"So who cuts your hair?" I ask, cracking up cuz Rock is bald.

"You got jokes, huh?" Rock says, clicking on his clippers. "My wife cuts my hair. What you got to say about that?"

"Cool," I say, shrugging.

"Yeah, it's cool," he says. "So what kind of cut you want?"

"Um, I don't know," I tell him. "Maybe like Sneaky's?" Sneaky has a pretty nice high top with a few ziggy lines on the sides.

"Like Sneaky's?" Rock shakes his head. "Nah, man, we gonna give you something that's all you, aight?"

I nod, but I have no idea what kind of haircut to ask for. Rock starts picking out my hair, and I grit my teeth as he cuts through all the naps.

"I know just what I'm gonna do," Rock says, more to himself than me. My head's on fire by the time he puts the pick down and buzzes on the clippers. Fluffy clumps of hair fall down like black snowflakes, and it gives me an idea of something to write about in Daddy's poem notebook.

"So what's up with you, man? How's your moms?" asks Rock.

"She's okay," I say, even though I'm not so sure.

"That's good. You takin' good care of her, right?"

"Yeah."

"And I bet you're excited for the summer, huh?" Rock switches clippers. "You and Sneaky gonna be in all kinds of trouble."

"Nah," I say. "I'm doing things on my own."

"You my hero, Isaiah," he laughs. "I wanna be just like you when I grow up!"

"You already grown up, Mr. Rock," I say.

"Yeah, and if I had been puttin' in work like you are when I was your age, I'd be grown up *and* a millionaire right now!"

"I'm not no millionaire," I say, thinking about the stolen sock.

"Not yet, li'l man," Rock says. "But you will be one day."

"I'ma buy a gigantic house," I say right away.

"You and me both," Rock says. He tells me about how he used to watch his big brother cut hair and dreamed of doing it himself one day.

"The very first cut I did was on my brother," Rock tells me. "And I jacked him up pretty bad!"

"Aww, man! Was he mad?" I ask. Antwan would probably destroy Sneaky if he ever messed up his hair.

"If he was, he didn't show it," Rock says, turning the chair to the left. "He just showed me what I did wrong, and went bald for a few weeks."

Rock cuts my hair pretty fast, and when he hands me the

mirror to check it out, my mouth drops open. He definitely doesn't mess up anymore.

"Yo, this is tight!" I say. Rock gave me a Mohawk that's way better than Sneaky's high top.

"You like that?" Rock grins. "Everybody's gonna be comin' in here asking for a haircut like *Isaiah's* now!"

"Thanks," I tell him, checking out every mirror.

"You got it," Rock says, grabbing the broom to sweep up my hair. "That right there is a 'Isaiah Dunn, Superhero' cut."

I freeze and stare at Rock, wondering if he knows about Daddy's stories. His back's to me as he's sweeping, and I'm just about to ask him when the shop door opens and a few older guys come in.

"'Ay, Rock, you got time for a quick edge-up?" asks one of them. The other guy looks at me, still standing in front of the mirror.

"Rock, you just did this cut?" he asks. "I gotta bring my little man in to get a cut like this!"

Rock winks at me, like, "Toldja," before answering the guys. He hands me the broom, and me and my superhero haircut get back to work.

May 28

THE SUITCASE BY the couch stops me cold.

I just woke up and wandered into the living room, and it's sitting there, nice and neat and ready to go. I guess we're leaving Miz Rita's after all. But to go where? I pray to God it's not back to Smoky Inn.

"Mama?" I call. She answers from the room she and Charlie have been sleeping in, Shayna's room. I go inside, stomach bouncing all over the place. Mama's sitting cross-legged on the bed, and she's holding Charlie's hands. She smiles when I come in, but it's a forced smile.

"Isaiah, come sit with us," she says. I walk closer but don't sit down.

"Are we leaving?" I ask. Mama grabs my hand. She tries to smile again, but her eyes are filling with tears.

"No, baby, you're not leaving," she says, her gaze going from me to Charlie.

"Goodie!" Charlie grins. "I like Miz Rita's house."

I stare right at Mama. I'm not four, like Charlie, and I notice she didn't say "*We're* not leaving." Mama's eyes find mine.

"But Mama is leaving."

"I knew it!" I explode. "I heard you guys!"

"Isaiah, calm down. Let me finish," Mama says. She grips my

hand even though I try to pull away. I hate that I feel tears on my cheeks. They match the ones on Mama's.

"It will only be for a month or so," Mama says in a shaky voice that gets stronger the more she talks. "I have to go away so I can get better. You want Mama to get better, don't you?"

"But you *are* better!" I say. "Miz Rita's helping! You don't have to go!"

Because Mama's crying, and I'm crying, Charlie starts crying.

"Mama, don't go away!" Charlie wraps her arms around Mama, and I can tell she's squeezing tight.

"Oh, baby, I don't want to leave you guys," Mama says.

"Then don't!" I say.

"I have to," Mama whispers.

"Why, Mama?" asks Charlie.

But I already know why.

"It's cuz of those bottles, right?" I ask. "Does Miz Rita know?"

Mama nods. "She knows. And you two are gonna stay here with her while I get . . ." Mama pauses and takes a deep breath. "While I get help."

Mama tells us about this place called Sunrise Recovery Center, where she'll be for the first part of the summer. It's a few hours away, in the middle of nowhere, and she says once she's there, they'll help her deal with a lot of things, more than just her drinking.

"I miss Daddy so, so much," she says, and wipes the extra tears that fall down. "This program will help me deal with missing him."

"I miss him, too, Mama," Charlie says excitedly. "So I should go with you, right?"

"No, baby." Mama smiles. "This place is just for mamas. It'll help me be a better mama to both of you. I want that more than anything right now."

"Oh," Charlie says. "Can I have some popcorn? Miz Rita said I could have some after I got dressed."

Mama gives Charlie a big kiss and hug, and tells her she can go get popcorn. Then it's just me and her. This time, when Mama tugs my arm, I sit down beside her. Her hand is warm when she touches my face, where all the stupid tears are.

"Isaiah," she says, "you're my li'l soldier, you know that?"

I don't say anything. I'm not a very good soldier if she has to leave to get better. A good soldier would be able to make things better, be a hero. That's what Daddy would want me to do.

"I'm very proud of you," Mama says. "You're an amazing big brother and the best son I could ever want."

"I'm the only son, Mama," I say.

"Even better!"

Mama tells me to do what Miz Rita says and not get in any trouble with Sneaky.

"I won't," I tell her. In my head, I'm imagining how shocked she'll be when she comes back and sees all the money I'll have.

"One more thing," Mama says, reaching under the bed. She pulls out a box, and I know what it is before I even look inside. "I had to go to the storage unit and get some things. Thought you might wanna do some reading this summer."

I tell Mama thanks and start taking out the notebooks. Daddy's notebooks. I flip through the pages, hoping none of them are blank. Mama even picks one up and starts reading. We stay like that for a while, reading Daddy's words together until some of the sad disappears.

May 29

LAST MEMORIAL DAY, Daddy barbecued on our tiny balcony, and Mama fussed at him the whole time about charcoal grills not being allowed. This year, I'm riding in the back of the car with Sneaky, feeling awkward and quiet all the way to McReynolds Park. I think about Mama, wonder what she's doing, if she's feeling better yet. I bet she's worse, cuz she doesn't have me and Charlie with her. That's how I am without her. Worse.

Sneaky's mom knocked on Miz Rita's door this morning, talkin' 'bout how she wanted me to go with them to the park for a barbecue. I tried to give Miz Rita my please-say-no look, but it didn't work. She was all like, "That sounds lovely; Sneaky ain't been around in forever!"

So here I am, sitting next to my ex–best friend and not sayin' one word. Sneaky mostly stares out of his window, but he also peeks over at me a few times. Sneaky's mom is listening to Jesus music, and Antwan, who's in the front seat with his headphones, looks annoyed. The lady on the song keeps sayin' something about the breath of life, and that's when Sneaky grins at me with this mischievous look on his face.

"Hey, Ma," he says, "what do you do if the breath of life stinks?"

I snicker, and even though Antwan rolls his eyes and looks even more annoyed, I can see his lip twitch into a smile, just a tiny bit.

"Boy!" Sneaky's mom gives him a look in the rearview mirror and swerves a little bit.

"Dang, Ma, watch the road!" Antwan complains, hunching over even more.

"Hush!" Sneaky's mom says, turning up her music. Antwan groans, probably because there's no way he can hear his music now.

"Dare you to get in the water when we get there," Sneaky says. "Five bucks if you get in!"

"Whatever," I tell him. Sneaky doesn't just give away money. He still owes me from our basketball game, but I don't say anything. And when we get to the park, I run into the water anyway. It's freezing cold!

"Oh, snap! You actually got in!" Sneaky says, and he has no choice but to come in, too. It's cool to do something before him for once. I splash him good when he sticks his feet in the water, then run out before he can get me back.

"Y'all crazy behinds got in that water?" Sneaky's mom is setting up chairs and blankets, and she shakes her head when we come over shivering. "Sneaky, don't come calling me when you catch pneumonia!"

She fusses for a bit, but makes Antwan go back to the car to get the towels she has in the trunk.

"Y'all dumb," Antwan says when he tosses us the towels. He spots a few of his friends, and they all sit on picnic tables doing nothing. I wonder if me and Sneaky will be like that when we're fifteen.

"So why you always with Angel now?" Sneaky asks, picking blades of grass and tossing them into the air. "You like her or something?"

"No!" I say real quick. "I mean, she's aight."

"But y'all got a business and stuff?"

"Yeah," I say. I don't tell him what the business is, exactly.

"Still gonna use your money for a new place?"

"Why you hangin' with those dudes?" I ask, kinda ignoring Sneaky's question. "Alex and all them?"

Sneaky shrugs. "I don't know. They cool, though. They 'bout the money like me."

"Yeah, I know," I say. "Cuz they stole *my* money. Did you know that?"

Sneaky's face twists into a question mark.

"Huh?"

"Alex is Angel's cousin. He told her him and his friends took the money from my backpack."

"The money for your place?"

"Yeah."

"Maaaan." Sneaky's face gets mad now. "I swear, I ain't know that, 'Saiah."

I look at him hard, trying to believe him. Sneaky wouldn't let nobody get away with doing that. Right?

"Watch and see what happens to him," Sneaky says. His voice is scary, kinda like Antwan's, and when I look over at Antwan and his friends, I know I never want us to be like them.

"You don't have to do nothing," I say. "Me and Angel gonna make it all back."

Me and Sneaky don't say anything for a while; he keeps picking grass and throwing it, and I keep watching the ripples in the water when boats pass by. A dog jets right by us, chasing some kind of toy. When it howls and barks, I think about Daddy.

Daddy always used to call McReynolds Park "Bark Park," because every time we went, no lie, there'd be a dog there barking. Daddy would say, "Okay, 'Saiah, if we get through the whole time with no dogs barking, I'll give you a dollar."

"Yo," Sneaky says after a while, "I ain't mean to be all crazy about the talent show. I'm just sayin', everybody there was WACK, and I know we coulda killed it! Why you ain't come?"

"It wasn't my fault," I tell him. "We got kicked out the Smoky Inn."

"For real? And then y'all went to Miz Rita's?"

I shake my head.

"Then where'd y'all go?"

"The car."

Sneaky's eyes get big. He gets it now.

"You coulda just stayed with us," he says, which feels like his "I'm sorry."

"I know, right?"

"I hope your mom gets better." Sneaky holds out his fist, and I dap it. Then we do our special handshake, laughing as we add even more parts to it.

"Hey, who's that?" I ask Sneaky when some dude walks over to our spot carrying a grill. He gives Sneaky's mom a hug. Sneaky sucks his teeth.

"Man, that's some dude," he says. "My mom's friend or something."

The guy sets up his grill and starts getting out hot dogs and stuff. He nods over at us.

"Hey, Aaron," the guy calls.

"Maaaan!" Sneaky groans and shakes his head. I laugh. Nobody calls Sneaky by his real name, except my mama, which is weird.

"My bad, my bad," the guy says, holding up his hands like we're the police. "Sneaky."

It sounds funny when he says it, like it doesn't fit.

"Hey," Sneaky says.

"Who's your buddy?" asks the guy.

"Isaiah."

"What's up, Isaiah?" says the guy. "You got a nickname, too? Or is it just Isaiah?"

"Isaiah."

"Good to meet you, Isaiah. I'm Wes."

"Hey," I say.

"Salvation of the Lord."

"Huh?" This Wes dude is kinda crazy.

"That's what your name means," Wes says. "Salvation."

"Maaan!" Sneaky groans again. He whispers to me, "She met him at my grandma's church. Crazy, right?"

"Yeah," I say. But I keep thinking about what he said, even while me and Sneaky try to spy on Antwan and his friends, and they end up chasing us and trying to throw us in the water. I think about it when we're stuffing our faces with hot dogs and potato salad and baked beans, and when we're just chillin', sippin' on root beers.

The only time I stop thinking about what my name means is when we're playing catch with the football Wes brought, and I hear a dog bark. Then I think of Daddy, and the dollar I won't be getting from him.

June 2

LAST DAY OF school, which means everybody's being all nice and wanting to sign each other's memory books.

In class, Mrs. Fisher makes sure we clean up our area and get the room looking decent. She also gives us time to write messages to each other. Most people write stuff like *nice knowin' ya,* and *we in middle school now!* At lunch (which is a bunch of gross leftovers) Sneaky writes, *Bro$ 4 life!* and draws a picture of a sneaker with dollar bills coming out of it. Angel writes *@DP,* which I know is code for our business name. I write my "In Common" poem in her book and sign my name all fancy.

"That's gonna be worth money one day," I tell her.

"Whatever," she says with a smile.

*   *   *

Miz Rita picks me up after school and says she'll stop by the library on the way home.

"This ain't gonna be a lazy summer, I can tell you that!" she says.

While Miz Rita takes Charlie to look at baby books, I head over to see Mr. Shephard.

"Look who's here!" Mr. Shephard says, giving me dap. "What's up, stranger?"

"Hey, Mr. Shephard," I say.

"Where you been, kid?" he asks. I tell him about my hustle at the barbershop, and he shakes his head.

"You dissed me for a job at a barbershop?"

"It's not like that!" I say, but I can tell Mr. S is joking.

"Well, your table's open," he says, pointing over toward the window. "Where's the notebook?"

"In my bag," I say. And there's no way I'm putting my bag down this time.

"Remember, just because it's summer doesn't mean you have to stop reading," Mr. Shephard says.

"I know," I say. I tell him I've also been busy writing my own stuff.

"Good. Since you're here, you should sign up for our summer reading program," Mr. Shephard says. I follow him to the front desk, and he gives me this plastic game board and a bag of Velcro pieces.

"Each time you read a book, you put on one of these." Mr. Shephard points to a star. "You read a book on our list, and you put on a sun. When you come to the library once a week for our programs, you stick on a beach ball. We add everything up in August and give out prizes."

The game board says "Ride the Reading Wave" and has a book on a surfboard. Kinda corny, but at least the prizes look cool.

"I mostly read my dad's notebooks," I say.

"Tell you what, since you and your dad are famous around here, we'll count that," Mr. Shephard says. "But you should check out some of the books on our list, too."

I take Mr. Shephard's advice and pick a book called *Bud, Not Buddy,* cuz the boy on the front kinda looks like Sneaky. When I go to my table and start reading, I find out Bud, the main guy in the story, is away from his mama like I am, only his mama died. That makes me pray that God won't ever let Mama die.

The story's good, and by the time Miz Rita's ready to go, I've already read two whole chapters. I tell Miz Rita, and she's so impressed, she forgets about making me do a research report for her. Charlie's got stickers on her shirt and a few books in her hand.

"Look at my books, 'Saiah!" she says, putting them all up in my face.

"I see, Charlie, dang," I tell her.

"Can you read one to me?" she asks.

I'm about to say no, but then I remember that picture books are super easy to read, and I can add up a whole lotta stars on my board by reading to Charlie.

"Yeah," I tell her. "I'll read 'em all!"

June 6

"SO HOW'S THE summer going, li'l man?" Rock asks me.

"It's good," I say. I spray his mirrors and wipe them down so they're sparkling clean.

"How's your writing coming along?" Rock asks. Man, ever since he caught me writing something in Daddy's notebook while I was waiting for Mama, he's been asking me the same question all the time.

"Okay," I tell him. "Wanna hear one of my poems?"

"Yeah, man, put it on me!" says Rock. I tell him my poem about the broken elevator at Miz Rita's place.

> *Broke up,*
> *Broke down,*
> *Don't get on*
> *Unless you wanna stick around.*
> *Smells like a bathroom,*

Moves like a snail.
Being on this elevator
Is like being in jail.
Stuck with stinky people,
Or dudes you do not know.
You gotta watch the ceiling
So the awkwardness don't show.
Broke down,
Broke up,
I got on,
There goes my luck!

Rock cracks up and tells me it's good.

"I can do one for you, too," I say. "That's my other business, you know."

Rock puts his clippers down and stares at me.

"What'cho mean, your other business, 'Saiah?"

I tell him about @Dunn Poems and how we sell poems. I'm thinking Rock's gonna be excited, but he just stares at me some more.

"You want me to sweep now?" I ask.

"Nah, no sweeping," Rock says. He pats his barber chair. "Have a seat."

Dang, another talk? Rock pulls up a stool and sits across from me.

"What's goin' on, li'l man?" he asks. "Every time I talk to you, you got a new hustle."

"I'm saving up," I tell him. "You said I was a throwback kid, remember?"

"Yeah, that's what I said," Rock chuckles. "The candy hustle was cool, even what you're doing in the shop. But you worryin' me, kid. What ten-year-old runs around selling poems on the spot?"

"Isaiah Dunn," I tell him. "Superhero."

"Superhero, huh." Rock shakes his head. "All I'm sayin' is, you gotta take time to be a kid, right?"

I shrug.

"Your daddy would want that."

When Rock says that, I freeze.

"Yeah, I knew Gary Dunn," he continues. "Only dude around who used to get his hair cut while writing in a notebook."

"He came here for haircuts?" I ask.

"Yeah, until he decided to take it all off," Rock laughs.

I remember Daddy joking that his hair line was marching backward like a college band at halftime. He even wrote a pretty funny poem about it.

"Now, I didn't know him real good or anything, but I know he loved his family," Rock says. "And you know what he said about writing?"

"No."

"He said words were little legacies that stay around much longer than he would."

"So?" I say. "I'd rather have Daddy than his words, and so would Mama!"

"I get it," Rock says. "But just remember, you got a lotta power in those notebooks you always carry around and don't want nobody to see. You carrying around your dad's legacy. And that's just as important as you trying to hustle up money and be the man of the house."

"But Daddy would want me to help Mama," I tell Rock.

"Money ain't the only way you can help her," Rock says. "It's not your job to be your dad. You being Isaiah is enough to make her proud, and your dad would be proud, too. Just think about it, okay?"

"Okay."

"Aight, now I want you to get outta here." Rock stands up and pulls a ten-dollar bill from his pocket. He snaps it before handing it to me. "This is for *you,* okay? Hang with your friends, go see a movie, get an ice cream cone or something, man."

I pocket the cash and tell Rock thanks.

"Hey, if I find out you didn't spend this money on something fun, I'ma cut your hair bald like your daddy!" Rock calls after me.

I laugh and take Rock's advice. I decide to walk home so I don't have to bug Miz Rita. On the way, I stop by the dollar store and get myself a gold notebook like Daddy's and a new pack of pens.

In my room at Miz Rita's, I finally write my first story ever, "Inka and the Secret of the Magic Mohawk."

It's hard, and it takes a long time. I still like poems better, but I'm glad I tried something new. When I put *my* gold notebook right next to Daddy's, I can almost feel him being proud of me. Guess Rock was right.

June 7

MAMA'S FIRST LETTER comes today, and I read it real slow.

Dear Isaiah,

I miss you so much! Leaving you and Charlie was the hardest thing I ever had to do. Yeah, I know you guys don't think I had to, but I did. I hope that as you get older, you understand. I'm doing better, and as they tell me, one day at a time. How is your summer going? Are you and Sneaky staying out of trouble? You betta not be giving Miz Rita a hard time! I can't wait to see you! You are an awesome son!

Love you always,
Mama

I start to fold the letter up, but then I get a better idea. I open Daddy's notebook, and I put Mama's letter there, so her words are next to Daddy's. I decide to write Mama a letter back.

Hey, Mama,

Thanks for the letter, but it was kinda short! I read a lot now, you know. Haha! Don't worry, me and Charlie are being good. I'm having a good time working with Rock, and I even started a new business with a girl from my school. (No, Mama, it's not like that!) We sell poems, and they're pretty good. I'll send you some. Well, gotta go, Miz Rita says we gotta go to her church. When are you coming back?

Love, your son,

Isaiah

I feel bad for sending Mama a short letter back, but I can't think of anything else I want to say. I could tell her about me and Sneaky, but I don't want that to make her worry. Plus, at least we're friends again, even if it's not *exactly* the same as before.

I take my letter to the living room, where Miz Rita is sitting with Charlie.

"Miz Rita, am I allowed to send Mama a letter?" I ask.

"Of course, baby," Miz Rita says. "You can write her whenever you want."

"Can I write her, too?" Charlie asks. "I wanna send her a picture!"

"Yes, baby, I'm sure your mama would love a picture from you."

While Charlie gets her crayons and paper, I put a PS on Mama's letter and tell her about the reading program at the library, and how I'm gonna get the biggest prize for reading so many books.

In a few minutes, Charlie bounces into the room and shows me her picture.

"You like it?"

"Uh, it's cool," I tell her. She drew a picture of me, her, Mama, *and* Daddy. I stare at the picture of Daddy and wonder if Charlie still doesn't get it.

"Oh, I forgot something!" Charlie grabs the picture and draws something else. When she hands it back to me, there's two more smiling stick figures.

"It's Miz Rita and Shayna!" Charlie says, grinning big. "Will Mama like it?"

Miz Rita tells her Mama will love it, but Charlie looks at me and asks the exact same question. I don't need a bowl of magic beans and rice to tell me how to answer.

"Yeah, Charlie, she will," I say. "Probably more than my letter."

June 9

"YO, IT'S SOCK man!"

I hear the voice as soon as I walk into the children's section at the library, and when I turn around, a group of guys bust up laughing. All of them except for Sneaky. I glare at him, and he stares at the table. Why's he still hangin' with them?

"You got any more socks in that bag?"

I recognize one guy from school but don't know his name. I also see Angel's cousin Alex. His friend nudges him, and they all laugh some more.

My chest is getting tight, but my feet take me right over to the table.

"What you say?" I ask.

"Nothin'."

"I know y'all stole my stuff!" My voice is pretty loud, and I hear the "shhhs!" right away.

"What's wrong with you?" says Alex.

"Yeah, shhh! It's the library!" says the guy from my school. He smirks.

Everybody's laughing, pretending that they don't know what I'm talking about. But I know they did it. Sneaky does, too, but he doesn't say anything.

"What you gonna do, candy boy?"

I decide in a second to do what Angel would do. I ball my

fist up and swing as hard as I can. Everything feels like it's in slo-mo. I see Sneaky's eyes get big, and the guy from my school isn't expecting my fist to meet his face.

But then somebody grabs my arm.

"Whoa, whoa! Isaiah, what's going on?"

"They stole money from me!" I yell, snatching away from Mr. Shephard.

"You lyin'!" says one of the guys, standing up.

"*Hey,* you need to sit down," Mr. Shephard says, pointing at the guy.

"They took the money from my backpack," I tell Mr. Shephard, ignoring the mean mugs they're giving me.

Mr. Shephard waves the security guard over and tells the guys he's glad the library has cameras they can go back and look at.

"Aww, man," says the guy from my school, making a face.

While the guard deals with the thieves, Mr. Shephard walks me to a small room and unlocks the door.

"Look, Isaiah, why don't you calm down in here. I'll be right back, okay?"

I throw my backpack on the floor and kick one of the boxes in the room. That makes me feel pretty good, so I kick another box. And another. Pretty soon, there are boxes everywhere.

"Well, at least you're taking it out on the box and not that guy's face," Mr. Shephard says when he comes into the room.

"Sorry," I say.

"It's all good," Mr. Shephard says. He sits on one of the boxes, so I do, too. "Why didn't you tell me you had something stolen here at the library?"

I shrug. Mr. Shephard probably doesn't know the rules when it comes to snitching. Mr. Shephard asks me how much money was stolen, and he whistles when I tell him.

"That's not chump change, Isaiah," he says.

"I was saving up."

Mr. Shephard sighs. "It's gonna be all right; we'll get it all figured out."

"Do you guys really have cameras in the library?" I ask. I'm pretty sure I picked my nose a few times at my table by the window.

Mr. Shephard grins.

"We do have cameras," he says, "but I'm not sure we'd still have the footage from mid-May."

"Aww, man, then we have no proof!" I say, wondering why Mr. Shephard is still smiling.

"Are you kidding me? They're out there confessing right now. It's a secret librarian trick to mention cameras," he says, holding up his fist for dap. I think about something else.

"Sneaky wasn't one of the dudes who took my money," I tell Mr. Shephard.

"Are you sure?"

"Yeah, he wasn't here that day."

Mr. Shephard nods and stands up. "Give me one sec."

When he comes back, Sneaky's with him. I'm both happy and mad to see him, so I just stare at him hard.

"I'll let you two have some space," Mr. Shephard says, patting Sneaky's shoulder before leaving the doorway.

"Dang, why you look like that?" Sneaky asks.

"You still hangin' with them? You sure you didn't help them take my money?"

"What?" Sneaky frowns. "Why you think that? I already told you I didn't know."

"Then why you—" I stop talking when Sneaky reaches in his bag and pulls out a video game case. He glances around before showing me.

"I told you to watch and see what happens, bro," Sneaky says with a grin. "I don't know how much you'll get, but you can take it to GameStop or put it on eBay or something."

"How you get this?" I ask, also wondering how Sneaky knew Alex bought a game with my money. Guess Alex runs his mouth to everybody.

"Hey, the master can't tell his secrets," Sneaky says. He holds his fist out, and before I know it, we're doing the candy boy shake.

"Looks like you two are having way too much fun," Mr. Shephard says, clapping his hands when he comes into the room.

"Can you dance *and* work? I mean, looks like you caused another fight in here, so the least you can do is restack the boxes, right?"

"Yeah," I say. Sneaky groans, but he says yeah, too.

"What is this room for, anyway?" Sneaky asks.

"Storage for now," Mr. Shephard says. "My guess is they'll use it for a meeting room."

Mr. Shephard tells us he'll be back in a few, and me and Sneaky get to work rearranging the boxes.

"Think he's gonna pay us for this?" Sneaky asks. He definitely *doesn't* like working if no money is involved.

"Nah," I say.

"Yo, were you really gonna hit Dontrel if library dude didn't grab you?" he asks.

"Yeah," I tell him. Sneaky looks proud.

"I woulda had your back," Sneaky says. "You know that, right?"

I didn't know it for sure, but it feels good to hear Sneaky say it.

I don't get The Idea about the library room until I'm at Miz Rita's, reading Charlie one of the Isaiah Dunn stories. It's about how Isaiah gets locked out of the Beans and Rice Room, where he goes for his superhero meal. The Idea hits me so hard, I stop reading, and Charlie elbows me.

"'Saiah, keep reading!"

"Sorry, Charlie," I say, closing Daddy's notebook and jumping up to get mine. "I gotta do something else right now! I'll finish the story soon!"

"Promise?"

"Promise!"

Charlie runs off to bother Miz Rita, and I open my notebook to a blank page and write in huge letters: *The Gary Dunn Writing Room.* The letters aren't perfect and bubbly like Angel's, but it's enough to get started.

June 10

IT'S SATURDAY, BUT I'm at the library before it even opens. As soon as I see Mr. Shephard, I tell him exactly what we should do with the storage room.

"Hmmm," Mr. Shephard says, his thinking face on. "It's actually a great idea, Isaiah; something the library would be proud to do."

Mr. Shephard says they had a big library meeting a few days ago and they talked about what to do with the room.

"Like I said before, there was the idea of turning it into a small meeting space that people could rent," Mr. Shephard says. "But someone also suggested a study room. I think your idea fits perfectly with that. Let me make a few calls while you hang out, okay?" he says.

I nod, and wander around looking at books while he's gone. I grab the new Diary of a Wimpy Kid book and head to my table to start reading it. A few minutes later, Mr. Shephard comes over with a big grin.

"I just got off the phone with Mrs. Priest. Remember her?" he asks.

"Ummm, no?"

"The lady from the reception," Mr. Shephard says. "She gave you the award."

"Oh yeah!" I say. "She was sitting at our table!"

"Exactly. So I gave her a call and told her a special writer has a special idea for our room."

"What did she say?" I feel myself getting excited, and I have a feeling Mr. S is gonna say something good.

"She liked the idea! She wants to meet with the library director on Monday to go over details, but in the meantime, you've got some work to do!"

Mr. Shephard says I need to write a letter to the library council to explain my idea and why it'll be good for the library.

"That's easy," I say, and I head over to my table to start writing. Mr. Shephard comes over from time to time to read what I have, and when I'm done, I sit at one of the computers to type it up.

"Remind you of anything?" Mr. Shephard asks.

"Yup," I say, remembering how I typed up Daddy's story to enter it into the library contest.

"I think this might be your lucky computer," Mr. Shephard says.

I hope so.

I feel really proud when I print out my letter to the library. Mr. Shephard says he'll scan it to Mrs. Priest ASAP.

"Next thing we have to do is start sorting through the boxes in here," says Mr. Shephard when we head into the storage room. "Books over here, office supplies over there, and junk in that corner."

"Got it," I tell him, and start sorting. The more I move things around, the more I see how awesome the room will be. I'm hoping it'll be done by the time Mama comes home.

"Can't make promises there, Isaiah," Mr. Shephard says. "We'd have to work at superhuman speed."

I grin. That's just perfect! Isaiah Dunn, Superhero, and the Race Against Time.

June 13

ALL THE COMMERCIALS are sayin', "Get Dad what he *really* wants this Father's Day," and it makes me hate TV. I turn the channel each time a commercial comes on, and finally I just toss the remote to Charlie and go to my room. Sneaky's off visiting his grandparents for a few days, so I can't run up to his place. I just wish I could be somewhere that has no Father's Day. I read for a while, until Miz Rita pokes her head in and hands me the second letter from Mama. After I read it, I almost want to ball it up and shoot a Kobe jumper into the trash can.

Mama says she's doing good and has so much to do when she comes home, blah blah blah. But all I see is one part. She's coming on June 29. June 29 is seven days *after* my birthday. And Mama doesn't even say she's sorry that she'll miss it!

Miz Rita makes us turkey sandwiches for lunch, and though it tastes really good, I don't feel like eating.

"Well, go on and tell me," Miz Rita says after I take only a few bites.

"Huh?"

"You been mopin' around all morning," Miz Rita says, "so go on and tell me what's the matter. I'm old, so my mind-reading skills aren't what they used to be."

"Oh. Nothing." I take a bigger bite out of the sandwich, and crunch on the plain potato chips like they're the best thing ever.

"Ummm-hmmm." I can tell Miz Rita doesn't believe me. "I'm surprised you ain't running off to the library today. Been going almost every day this week!"

That's just it! I've been working hard at the library, clearing out the room for Mama's surprise, and she won't even be here for my birthday!

"I wanna go to the library!" Charlie says. She sprays my arm with potato chip crumbs. Gross!

"No talkin' and eatin', baby," Miz Rita tells Charlie. Then she looks at me. "If it makes you feel any better, my friend Ida can't stop talkin' about the poem you wrote her. She says you real talented."

That does make me feel better.

"Can you write a poem for me, Isaiah?" asks Charlie. This time, no food comes flying out her mouth.

"You can stand in line, little girl," Miz Rita jokes, "cuz he gotta do one for me first!"

So that's how we spend the afternoon: no more Father's Day commercials or Mama-missing-my-birthday letters. Just me writing poems about Charlie's Afro puff and Miz Rita's yummy pound cake. And lots of laughs.

June 19

WHEN I TELL Angel I gotta put @Dunn Poems on hold while I work on the library project, she don't even trip, like maybe Sneaky would have. She says she'll help. We get the room pretty much cleared out, and then there's the yucky stuff like sweeping the floor and getting rid of the cobwebs.

"You'll never guess what just happened!" Mr. Shephard says. He's more hyped than I've ever seen him, so it's gotta be great news.

"I just got off the phone with Mason Crew Collections, which is a furniture store," Mr. Shephard says. "Long story short, they have a bunch of furniture they can't use, and they want to donate to the room!"

"For real?" asks Angel. She frowns at a few cobwebs on the ceiling. "They wanna come and clean this up, too?"

Mr. Shephard laughs. "You guys have done a good job. We can have our custodians finish this tonight. The company wants to start tomorrow with putting in carpet. Things are moving fast now, my friends!"

"Superhuman fast," I tell him.

June 22

WHEN I WAKE up, I feel exactly the same as I did yesterday, even though I'm eleven now. Last year, Daddy made me a huge breakfast in bed: ten pancakes, ten pieces of bacon, ten bananas, and ten little cups of orange juice. Of course, I couldn't eat everything, but Mama, Daddy, and Charlie helped me.

I throw on some shorts and a T-shirt and walk to the kitchen. No fancy birthday breakfast. I pour a bowl of cereal instead and ask Miz Rita if I can go to the library since Rock says he won't need me at the shop today. Usually she wants to know if someone is going with me or how long I'll be or if I would rather she drive me over. Today she says yes without even asking any questions. She doesn't even say "Happy Birthday."

The room at the library is almost perfect. I help Mr. Shephard hang pictures on the walls, and some of those pictures are quotes from Daddy's notebooks. It feels a little weird to see Daddy's words so big, but it's also really cool.

"The desks come in tomorrow, Isaiah," Mr. Shephard says. "And the computers will be delivered early next week."

Mr. Shephard says my idea touched a lot of hearts, and companies have reached out to Mrs. Priest because they want to donate whatever they can to make the room nice. I'm counting down the days till Mama gets back and hoping she'll be as excited about the room as I am.

Mr. Shephard and I spend some time arranging the green beanbags and putting books on the bookshelves. Just when I realize how hungry I am, somebody taps me on the shoulder.

"Yo, you at the library on your *birthday*?"

I whirl around and see Sneaky standing there with a smirk on his face.

"What's up, Sneaky?" I say. We do our special handshake, and I tell him about the project. He thinks it's cool.

"I mean, cool for people who like to be at the library," he says. "You guys gonna put a vending machine in here? Cuz if you're not . . ."

"No candy sales in the library," Mr. Shephard says with a smile. I've told him about Sneaky's hustle, but it's not gonna fly in the library.

"Aww, man! You sure about that?" asks Sneaky, turning on his businessman swag. "I mean, you probably would get way more kids in here if you let me sell candy. Kinda like Girl Scout Cookies, but better."

When Mr. Shephard doesn't budge, Sneaky says, "Well anyway, Miz Rita said to tell you to come home."

"Serious?" I make a face. "I need to finish up in the room."

"Her rules." Sneaky shrugs.

I tell Mr. Shephard I'll be back, and he gives me the thumbs-up. Sneaky says his mom will take us to the movies later on, and since it's my birthday, I get to pick the movie.

"But, dude, no more *Finding Dory*," he says with a straight face. Charlie's been watching that nonstop, and Sneaky likes to tease that I'm really the one who keeps picking it. I punch him in the arm, and he chases me to the building.

"Hopefully you're not in trouble," Sneaky says when we get to Miz Rita's door. Man, I got grounded on my birthday once, and it was *not* fun.

When I open the door, though, I don't see trouble at all.

"SURPRISE!"

I look around the room and see Miz Rita and Charlie, Sneaky's mom, Angel, and even Rock and his wife. The whole living room is decorated, and everybody's smiling.

"We got you, 'Saiah!" Sneaky laughs. "Bet you thought everybody forgot, right?"

"Yeah," I say.

"I forgot, 'Saiah," says Charlie, hiding her face in her hands. "But then I remembered!"

I tickle her until she laughs all high like Elmo.

"Thanks, Miz Rita," I say, giving her a hug next.

"Of course, baby," she says, and she gives me a big kiss! Yuck!

Rock slaps me five so hard, it hurts.

"Let's have fun with eleven, aight, li'l man?"

Sneaky bets me a dollar I can't eat five slices of pizza, which is a mistake for him, cuz I do it easy. He actually gives me the dollar!

Right before Miz Rita brings out my cake, her phone rings. "Grab that for me, 'Saiah, okay?" she says.

I swipe the green check mark to answer the call. "Hello?"

"Isaiah?"

I almost drop the phone.

"Mama?"

"Happy birthday, baby!" she says, and I can hear the smiles in her voice. It's the best present ever!

"Thanks, Mama!" I say. "Miz Rita got me a cake with my face on it!"

"You guys make sure to take a picture of it for me," Mama says. I tell her if I had a cell phone I could take a picture of it easily, and she laughs a real laugh.

"I love you, baby, and I'm so proud of you. You've been so brave with everything that's going on," Mama says.

"You too, Mama," I say. I wanna tell her about the project sooooo bad, but I know it's gotta be a surprise.

Miz Rita puts the call on speaker so Mama can sing "Happy Birthday" with everyone else. Sneaky and Charlie sing mad loud and off-key, but my ears hold on to Mama's voice. I feel sad when we have to say goodbye, but I just keep imagining how excited Mama will be when she gets back.

I know I'm eleven now, but before I go to sleep, I make sure to tell Inka all about the library project and how I'm hoping it'll help Mama. It looks like she's smiling.

June 28

READY
Everything
Gotta be
Just right.
Dishes washed and floor swept and trash not a
mountain to climb.
Vacuum and scrubbing and dusting and
Trusting she's better.
She gotta be.
Haircut and Hair puff
And enough
food for everybody and they mama.
Also,
Heart beating fast and
Hoping that
we're ready.

June 29

I TRY TO hold Charlie back when we hear the front door unlock, but it's no use. She runs like a madwoman.

"MOMMEEEEEE!"

Charlie screams loud enough to have the whole building dialing 911, but today, nobody's telling her to shut up. I watch from the couch as Mama walks inside and then instantly has Charlie in her arms and a smile on her face. She looks different, but also the same.

"Charlie baby!" Mama squeezes Charlie and kisses her over and over. "Mmmmm, Mama missed you so much!"

"I missed you, too, Mama," Charlie says, her voice muffled in Mama's love.

I'm split between wanting them to hug forever and being ready for Mama to stop so she sees me. When she finally puts Charlie down, her eyes find me.

"Look at my big boy!" Mama says, squeezing me so tight, I can barely breathe. She kisses my cheek again and again and runs her hand over my fresh Mohawk.

"You got taller, 'Saiah," Mama says, and I guess she's right.

"How are you feeling, Mama?" I ask. Her face looks super happy.

"Good, baby," Mama says. "I'm feeling good. I'm glad to be home."

Mama tells us about the food at her program, and Miz Rita laughs and says it's a miracle she made it out alive.

"First thing I'm gonna make is some *real* banana pudding," Mama says.

"Can you make it today, Mama?" Charlie asks.

"Charlie, remember what Miz Rita told you!" I say, giving her a look.

"Oh yeah," Charlie says. Miz Rita's told us to make sure we let Mama ease into things, and not bug her with little stuff. If it was up to me, I'd take Mama to the library right away for my surprise. But we have a plan, so we have to wait.

After dinner, Charlie forgets all about what Miz Rita said, and begs Mama to watch *Finding Dory*.

"Yes, Charlie, we can watch it, but how 'bout after you take your bath?" Mama says.

"I'll help her," I volunteer. "You just sit down and relax."

Mama helps Miz Rita clean up in the kitchen instead, and Charlie takes the fastest bath ever. For the first time in a long time, Mama stays awake for the whole movie.

Once it's over, Miz Rita takes Charlie to read a story so I can have time alone with Mama, just like we planned.

"What's this?" Mama asks when I hand her a card.

"Just something to welcome you back," I tell her.

I watch her read my poem, and then the invitation that Angel created.

"July first at the library?" Mama raises an eyebrow. "Did you win another contest or something?"

"Nope!" I say. "Even better."

"I can't wait!"

Me either.

July 1

"YOU ALL RIGHT, Isaiah?" Mama asks, squeezing my hand. "You lookin' more nervous than me!"

"I'm good," I tell her, swallowing hard. I know the room is perfect, but what if it's not perfect enough to help Mama, to keep her from being sad? But then I think about how she'll see Daddy's words everywhere, and how they'll make her strong.

His words in my mind make me strong, too. *A head held high means you see everything you're supposed to!* There's no stomach karate when we walk into the library; I just keep my head high, hold on to Mama's hand, and smile.

We don't have to dress all fancy this time, but I wear one of Daddy's ties anyway. There's a big red bow in front of the room, and Mrs. Priest motions for me and Mama to come stand with her behind the bow. It's not a huge crowd at all, but people snap pictures like we're famous!

"Isaiah, what is this?" Mama whispers, her eyes wide.

"You'll see," I whisper back, grinning for the cameras.

"So good to see you both!" Mrs. Priest says, hugging me and Mama. Mama holds my hand the whole time. "I'll be short and sweet this time, okay, Isaiah?" I nod, and Mrs. Priest waves to get everyone's attention.

"Almost a year ago, a family lost a father, a husband, and a tremendous writer," Mrs. Priest says. "And were it not for a talented son who wanted to keep his father's legacy alive, the story would've ended there. But I'm here today to let you know the story is only beginning! Isaiah, you are a hero to your family, and we thank you for sharing your father's words with us. And to all of you who came out to celebrate with us, welcome to the official opening of the Gary Dunn Writing Room!"

Mrs. Priest hands me a giant pair of scissors, and me and Mama cut the bow together. Everyone claps and whistles.

"After you," Mrs. Priest says, and me and Mama walk into the room.

The room is green and brown and yellow, Daddy's favorite colors. Daddy's words hang on the walls, and there are six writing stations with brand-new computers. Yellow and green beanbags are in the corners of the room, and bookcases line the walls.

Mama's completely shocked as she walks around the room, touching each frame that holds Daddy's words. Charlie bounces on a beanbag and grabs a book.

" 'Saiah, can you read this to me?"

"Mama, you okay?" I ask, not wanting to let go of her hand.

"Yes, baby," she says, giving me a squeeze. "I am very okay."

Somebody from the paper takes a picture of me reading to Charlie and asks me what gave me the idea to have the writing room.

"I just wanted to make a cool place for people who want to write," I say.

"And do you think your dad would've done a lot of writing here?"

"Yeah, he would have," I say. Then I think for a second. "But now I'm gonna do the writing for him. And for me."

July 4

POP! POP! POW!

The fireworks are going off one after the next, and Miz Rita's complaining that she can't get a good picture of them on her phone.

"Just keep clicking, Rita," Mama advises with a chuckle. "You bound to get a good one somewhere in there."

"I like that one, 'Saiah!" Charlie says, pointing to the pink sparkles disappearing into the night.

"Nah, that one's better," Sneaky says when red, white, and blue lights explode.

The roof of our apartment building is the best place to watch fireworks, so that's where me, Mama, Charlie, Miz Rita, and Sneaky are. I watch Mama, who's sipping lemonade from the "Hot Mama" mug I got her last Christmas. Her and Charlie are wearing matching dresses that look like the flag, and they're both swatting at mosquitoes.

"Miz Rita, I don't think your bug spray is working," Sneaky says, squashing one on his arm.

Miz Rita shakes her head and sprays us some more. Nobody says anything about going inside. No way we're gonna miss this.

I feel words coming when the sky lights up with yellow and orange, so I open my notebook and catch them all.

"Listen to this one, Mama," I say once I'm finished.

> *"Twinkle twinkle,*
> *Little dream.*
> *You are closer*
> *Than you seem.*
> *You explode,*
> *But it's all good.*
> *Now I see you*
> *Like I should.*
> *Twinkle twinkle,*
> *Little dream.*
> *We are stronger*
> *Than we seem."*

When I look up, Mama's got this smile on her face, like she has a huge secret.

"You like it?" I ask. Mama nods.

"You know what I think, Isaiah?"

"What?"

"I think," she says, taking a sip from her mug and winking, "it's gonna be one of *them* years!"

Me and Mama fist-bump right as the sky explodes with gold sparkles.

"Nah," I tell her. "It's gonna be even *better.*"

ACKNOWLEDGMENTS

God, the Master Creative Author, has given me the gift of weaving words together in a way that hopefully brings transformation and inspiration to young people. You get the glory, and I am forever grateful.

Hulrick, I would not have pressed "submit" for the short-story contest if it had not been for your calming encouragement in the midst of pandemonium. Thank you for your support of my writing. . . . Your turn now! (Hint, hint, G.C. Drum-Off!) ☺

Bianca, Ricky, Micaiah, Natalia, and Zackery, you are my greatest chapters! Without you, I would never know how to write in situations of utter chaos. Now that you see this book thing is real, how about letting Mommy write in peace sometimes? ☺ I love you guys forever and hope I have shown you that working hard for your passion is always worth it. CHAMPION'S MOUNTAIN!

To my parents, thank you for reading to me, taking me to the library, and supporting my writing since I was little. I am beyond blessed to have you in my corner; that fact brings peace to my soul. I love you!

To Kim and Karmen, you guys are usually the first to read

my work, and I always appreciate your feedback. Thank you for being not only sisters but friends. I love you both!

To my brother, Pierre, I have waited my whole life for you! You were my brother the second you said you liked Kobe. (Good choice, Kim!) MAMBA FOREVER!

To my homies, Jayne and Afiya, it's so amazing to have friends who get that whole "Wait, you have *how* many kids?" thing. Let's keep holding it down, ladies; we haven't lost our minds, and we're doing a great job!

To Zaria, Zadan, Zani, and Zach, thanks for being best buddies with my children! The nine of you give me so much insight for my writing . . . sometimes more than I can handle!

To Mr. and Mrs. Usher, the best husband-and-wife teaching duo in the universe! You both watered the seeds of writing talent that you saw in me from long ago, and I hope you are proud as you watch those seeds grow. The educational foundation you gave me was invaluable, and it still grounds me to this day. I love you both!

To Dr. Bowe and my Oakwood family, best years of my life! I pray to come back and serve in some capacity.

Phoebe and Elizabeth, you two have been fantastic throughout each step of this process! Thank you for helping me navigate. Ellen, I'll never forget our talk at NCTE 17. Thank you for being a voice of urgency for me.

Gabrielle, thank you for your insights on this book. Look at what some Calvin Center kids did! ☺

Anyone who knows me well knows that I am a huge Kobe Bryant fan. I have come to believe that the five pillars of his famed Mamba Mentality—passion, obsession, relentlessness, resiliency, and fearlessness—can be applied to the pursuit of any task, dream, career, or hobby. Writing, in particular, requires all five, and the book you hold in your hands is the result of years of me writing just because I love it. It is the result of frustration, rejection letters, contest wins, discouragement, lost and broken jump drives, destroyed documents, joy, inspiration, and persistence. You are holding this book because I never gave up. So don't you give up either! Pursue your passions with wisdom and tenacity so that one day, I'll be holding your work—whatever it may be—in my hands!

ABOUT THE AUTHOR

Kelly J. Baptist's "The Beans and Rice Chronicles of Isaiah Dunn" won the inaugural We Need Diverse Books short-story contest and is included in the middle-grade anthology *Flying Lessons and Other Stories*. As a result of her work in an urban school district, Kelly felt compelled to continue Isaiah's story. *Isaiah Dunn Is My Hero* is her debut middle-grade novel. She is also the author of the picture book *The Electric Slide and Kai*. When she's not actually writing, Kelly is usually thinking about writing . . . and dreaming of palm trees while living in southwest Michigan. She keeps beyond busy with five amazing children, who always give her plenty of story ideas and background noise to write to.